DUKE

BLACKWINGS MC BOOK TWO

BY

TEAGAN BROOKS

Cathy

♡ Teagan Brooks

Dedication

To my readers.
Without you, this would still be a
document on my laptop.

Contents

PROLOGUE	1
CHAPTER ONE	12
CHAPTER TWO	16
CHAPTER THREE	27
CHAPTER FOUR	37
CHAPTER FIVE	45
CHAPTER SIX	58
CHAPTER SEVEN	64
CHAPTER EIGHT	72
CHAPTER NINE	80
CHAPTER TEN	88
CHAPTER ELEVEN	99
CHAPTER TWELVE	113
CHAPTER THIRTEEN	120
CHAPTER FOURTEEN	125
CHAPTER FIFTEEN	133
CHAPTER SIXTEEN	141
CHAPTER SEVENTEEN	152
CHAPTER EIGHTEEN	168
CHAPTER NINETEEN	188
CHAPTER TWENTY	193
CHAPTER TWENTY-ONE	198
CHAPTER TWENTY-TWO	207
CHAPTER TWENTY-THREE	213
CHAPTER TWENTY-FOUR	222
CHAPTER TWENTY-FIVE	231
CHAPTER TWENTY-SIX	236
CHAPTER TWENTY-SEVEN	243
CHAPTER TWENTY-EIGHT	250
CHAPTER TWENTY-NINE	263
CHAPTER THIRTY	268
CHAPTER THIRTY-ONE	279
EPILOGUE	288

PROLOGUE

Reese

Senior Prom Night

I didn't want to go. I honestly couldn't tell you why I agreed to go to prom with Jamie. He was a nice guy and he caught me on a good day. Before I knew what was happening, he had persuaded me to be his date. I had one condition, and I repeatedly stressed it; we were going as friends only. Every time I brought it up, he smiled and agreed.

The actual prom was okay, I suppose. I wasn't really into it, but I felt like it was something I might regret not doing later on in life, so I forced myself to go. Jamie was a perfect gentleman the entire night. I didn't know him very well. We had one or two classes together, but we never socialized outside of class. Frankly, I was shocked when he asked me to be his date. When I asked him why he asked me, his reply was, "You looked like you could use some fun." He was right about that, but I didn't comment on it any further.

When the dance portion of the evening was over, the school was hosting an after-prom party in the school's gymnasium. It sounded seriously lame, and I had no interest in going. I made myself attend the prom, but the after-prom was off the table. Jamie and I were dancing the last dance of the night when he asked, "Do you want to go to the after-prom party hosted by the school, or would you like to go to another party tonight?"

Another party? That got my attention. "Where's the other party?" I asked, trying not to sound too excited.

"At a friend of a friend's house. This guy has parties every weekend; it has nothing to do with prom."

I agreed to go with him, hoping it would prove to be fun. Carbon was gone on a run for the MC and wouldn't be back for two more days, which meant I didn't have a curfew.

When the song ended, I quickly changed clothes in the girls' locker room. I had bought a dress for after-prom in case we decided to go. It was a basic strapless bodycon dress in the same shade of green as my prom dress. Since I didn't have to change my shoes or any accessories, I was in and out in less than five minutes.

Jamie was waiting for me in the hallway. He had changed out of his tuxedo into a pair of worn jeans, a black t-shirt, and motorcycle boots. All he needed was a leather cut and he would look just like my brother. His eyes widened when he saw me. "Damn, Reese. I know we said just friends, but you look fucking hot as hell in that dress."

That caught me off guard. I wasn't trying to look hot and sexy. Honestly, I got the dress because it was cheap and it matched my shoes. "Oh, thanks. You look like you belong on a motorcycle," I said, hoping to redirect his attention away from me.

He smiled brightly, "One day soon, I hope."

Nope, I wasn't going there with him. If he asked me to prom because he had somehow figured out who my brother was, I didn't want to know. If he didn't know about Carbon, I wasn't going to tell him. He was obviously trying to get

3

in with the local MC, and I wanted nothing to do with that.

The party was being held at a house out in the middle of nowhere. Well, Croftridge itself was in the middle of nowhere, but there were parts that weren't completely secluded like this place. Nothing but fields and forest surrounded the rundown two-story house. A bonfire of sorts toward the back of the house had some people milling about while others were going in and out of the house at a steady rate.

I continued to survey the scene while Jamie parked the car. I didn't have a good feeling about this party, but I couldn't put my finger on what was unsettling to me. "How do you know this guy again?" I asked.

Jamie shrugged, "He's a friend of a friend. I don't know him that well, but my friends are here, so it's all good."

I followed him around the house to the bonfire. It didn't take him long to find his group of friends. Some I recognized from school, others I had never seen before. He introduced me to all of them before he left me to get us drinks. I was uncomfortable with the group of strangers and trying to think of something to say when I heard my name.

"Reese!" That definitely was not Jamie's voice, but it was one I recognized. One that sent a shiver down my spine.

Shit.

Shit.

Shit.

Duke. Tall, sexy, panty-melting Duke with his thick, dark brown hair and his icy, blue eyes. He was all man and had starred in several of my late night fantasies, not that I would ever admit it.

I tried to pretend like I didn't hear him, even though I had already jolted at the sound of my name. "Reese Walker! Get your ass over here right now, girl!" Oh, no the fuck he didn't. Sexy or not, I wasn't going to let him talk to me like that.

Duke

Phoenix sent me out to Ricky Reynolds's house to check out these weekend parties he started having about a month or so ago. The rumors around town were that he came into some money when his father passed away, but Phoenix wanted to be sure that was all he was up to. He suspected there was significant drug activity going on at Ricky's parties and wanted proof. Phoenix was hardcore against two things: drugs and abuse of any kind against women and children.

Sipping my beer, I leaned against the side of the house and watched the people around the bonfire. Thus far, I had only seen people drinking and a few smoking weed. What surprised me was that no one seemed to notice my presence. I walked into the house, grabbed a beer, and had been standing in the exact same spot for almost 45 minutes without a word from anyone.

My eyes landed on a girl with one hell of a body walking toward the bonfire. She seemed out of place in her short, tight green dress and strappy high-heeled sandals. Her caramel colored hair was a mass of curls that hung midway down her back. I desperately wanted her to turn around so I could see her face.

I kept my eyes on her and watched silently as she and a guy approached a group by the fire. I suspected the majority of that group was too young to be drinking, but kids will be kids and that's not why I was there. They talked with the group for a few minutes, and then the guy walked toward the house. The girl turned and looked back at him as he left. She didn't see me, but I clearly saw her.

"Reese!" I yelled. What in the fuck was Carbon's little sister doing at Ricky's party? If Carbon knew she was here, he would be pissed as hell. Reese tried to act like she didn't hear me, but I knew she did. I saw her stiffen when I yelled her name. "Reese Walker!" I yelled louder. "Get your ass over here right now, girl!"

That did it. She whirled around and glared at me. "Who in the fuck do you think you're talking to, Duke Jackson? I don't answer to you."

I ignored what she said and advanced toward her. "Does your brother know you're here?"

She put her hands on her hips and cocked one hip to the side. "It doesn't matter if he does or doesn't. I'm 18 years old, and I don't need his permission for anything."

That was bullshit, and she knew it. Yeah, she might be a legal adult, but she still needed Carbon's permission because she was living with him. Hell, she was still in high school. I heard him tell her on several occasions that he would ship her ass off to a boarding school or all girls college if she didn't behave. "I see. So, you wouldn't mind if I gave him a call right now to let him know your whereabouts?"

She stiffened, then sighed, "What do you

want, Duke?"

"You need to go home. Right now," I answered. If Phoenix was right and there were drugs coming from these parties, she didn't need to be anywhere near it. Besides, the majority of the people there were too old for her to be hanging around with anyway.

"I can't go home right now. We just got here, and my date, who is also my ride, has already started drinking," she explained.

Not a problem. "I'll take you home. Let's go."

She shook her head. "I can't get on your bike dressed like this," she gestured to the tight as fuck dress she had painted on her gorgeous body.

"You're in luck," I grinned and held up my keys. "I'm in a cage tonight. Now, let's go."

"I need to tell my date I'm leaving. Be right back." She turned and walked back to the boy she arrived with before I could say otherwise. When she got close, he slid his arm around her waist while she whispered in his ear. I decidedly did not like any of that one bit. I silently fumed while she spoke with him, smiling and laughing at the fucker. The muscle in my jaw started to tick when she leaned in and kissed him on the cheek. I'd had enough. I had taken two steps toward her when she pulled back and began walking in my direction.

She didn't say anything to me while we walked to my truck. She continued her vow of silence for the entire drive to Carbon's condo. I knew she was pissed. She sat there with her arms crossed and stared out the passenger window. When I pulled up to Carbon's place, she jumped out of the truck and whirled around, pinning me with her angry green eyes. "Thanks for ruining my prom night, asshole!" Then, she slammed the door and stomped off.

I climbed out of the truck and followed her. "Reese, wait." Did she? Of course not. She continued stomping to the front door. I carefully grabbed her arm and turned her around to face me. "It was your prom night?"

"That's what I said," she spat.

"For that, I'm sorry, but you had no business being at Ricky's party," I explained.

"What business did you have there, Duke?" she asked with an eye roll.

She answered her own question in unison with me, "Club business."

She turned around and unlocked the front door. I don't know why, but I followed her inside. "Are you going to be okay here by yourself?"

She rolled her eyes. "I'll be just fine, Duke. It's not the first time I've stayed by myself and I'm sure it won't be the last. Now, if you'll excuse me, I have to find Carbon's stash of liquor so I can salvage what's left of my prom night."

"What do you mean by that?" I asked.

"It's like a rite of passage, to get drunk on prom night," she looked at me incredulously.

"Hang on a second," I said and proceeded to do one of the stupidest things I've ever done. I walked out to my truck, unlocked the toolbox in the truck bed, and pulled out the bottle of tequila I had purchased earlier that day.

Walking back into Carbon's place, I held up the bottle and asked, "You got limes?"

She grinned. "Why Duke, are you offering to get me drunk on prom night?"

"Only because it's your prom night and I don't want you here alone drinking. If you're going to get trashed, you should have someone here with you."

That's how I ended up getting shitfaced with Carbon's little sister on her prom night. We took shot after shot. Before long, the bottle was half empty, and I was feeling great. We talked and laughed for hours. I was having a great time getting to know her better.

We were sitting on the sofa in the living room when she leaned closer to me and whispered, "Do you know what else is a rite of passage on prom night?"

I shook my head. I had no idea what she was talking about. I didn't go to prom when I was in high school. I was busy working and helping take care of my little sister. Reese climbed into my lap and straddled me. She leaned forward until her lips were only a hair's breadth away from mine and whispered, "Sex."

CHAPTER ONE

Reese

I woke with a nasty hangover. My head was pounding. The room was spinning. And there was a very good chance I was going to vomit all over myself if I didn't hurry and get myself to the bathroom.

I nearly fell on my ass when I tried to get out of bed, but I somehow managed to run a wobbly path to my bathroom. Dropping to my knees, I emptied the contents of my stomach in a rapid and violent fashion. When I was finished, I was covered in a light sheen of sweat, but aside from the taste in my mouth, I felt marginally better.

I carefully rose to my feet and grabbed my toothbrush. After brushing my teeth twice, I hopped in the shower. While I was washing my hair, bits and pieces of the previous night started coming back to me in flashes.

Duke.

I gasped and my eyes flew open, shampoo promptly running directly into my eyes. After squealing and rinsing away the shampoo, I focused my attention on trying to remember what happened. Duke took me home from the party. We argued. I wanted to get drunk, because that's what people do on prom night. Duke held up a bottle of tequila. After that, things got fuzzy. Obviously, I succeeded in my prom night quest of getting trashed, hence the wretched hangover, but my body felt sore, in a deliciously naughty way. I looked down and gasped when I saw the finger-shaped bruises on my hips. Twisting my body as far as I could, I saw a faint red handprint on my ass. Further inspection revealed a hickey on my inner thigh and what appeared to be beard burn on my breasts.

With each mark's discovery, the memories came pouring in. Duke squeezing my hips while I rode him. Duke slapping my ass while he took me from behind. Duke teasing me by sucking on my inner thighs before finally putting his mouth where I wanted it. Duke lavishing my breasts with attention from his mouth while he finger fucked me to orgasm.

Holy.

Fuck.

How many times did we fuck last night? More importantly, where in the hell was he? I started to panic. I needed to talk to him. He couldn't tell Carbon what happened. My brother would freak if he knew I fucked one of his club brothers in his house while he was out of town.

I quickly finished my shower and got dressed. There was no sign of him or his things in my room. I started to run down the stairs, but managed to get myself under control enough to walk down. If he was down there, I didn't want him to think I was running after him. I scanned the living room and found nothing. A quick sweep of the kitchen revealed he wasn't there. I opened up the front door and saw that his truck was gone.

I started to get angry, and then realized I had nothing to be angry about. I got what I wanted, and I had a good time doing it. I had no interest in being in a relationship with Duke. To be more accurate, I had no interest in being in a relationship with anyone. My last one had ended in the worst way, and I wasn't up for a repeat experience anytime soon, if ever. If he told

Carbon, well, I would deal with that when the time came. I shrugged off all thoughts of Duke and went about my day.

CHAPTER TWO

Duke

I wasn't worth a shit at work. I didn't have a hangover, but I couldn't think about anything other than Reese and everything we had done the night before. Never had I met a woman who was as compatible with me in the bedroom as she was. While some of the things we did were raw and dirty, it didn't feel like empty sex. It felt like more, at least to me it did, and I hoped she felt the same way. I shook my head. I was starting to sound like I had grown a pussy.

I finished up at work, took a quick shower, and headed over to Carbon's place. I knew he wasn't back from the run yet, so I didn't have to come up with a reason to be there. I rang the doorbell and waited. When no one answered the door, I knocked, then knocked a little harder a few minutes later. She didn't answer the door, and I didn't have her cell phone number. With nothing else to do, I went back to the clubhouse.

I stopped by Carbon's place the following day, but she didn't answer the door then either. I wasn't sure if she wasn't home or if she was avoiding me. I hoped it wasn't the latter. My mind got carried away, and I started to wonder if she regretted that night. She was drunk, but she wasn't incoherent. I know I asked her several times if she was sure she wanted to have sex with me. She repeatedly said yes. Normally, I wouldn't take a girl that had been drinking to bed, but I was drunk, too, and all rational thoughts ceased to exist when she said yes. It's not an excuse, just a fact.

It was a little over two weeks before I saw her again. I had been by Carbon's place several times under the pretense of hanging out with him just to try to catch a glimpse of her. She was like a ghost. Every time I was at his place, she was nowhere to be found. I couldn't ask Carbon about her without looking suspicious because, like the asshole I was, I had never asked about her before. I had just resigned myself to the fact that I would have to let it go, let her go, when she walked into the clubhouse in the middle of a shitstorm.

She was at the clubhouse for well over a day before I had the chance to really talk to her. I had stepped in between her and Carbon and asked her a few questions, but those pertained to the girl she brought to the clubhouse for help.

Finally, Dash and I caught Reese and her friend in the common room. Dash made it easy for me to talk to her by making a beeline for their table. I could tell he was interested in Reese's friend. Deciding to play the role of wingman, I asked the girls if they wanted to play a game of pool with us, directing my attention to Ember instead of Reese. To my surprise, Reese answered in agreement, and then, as luck would have it, her and I ended up on the same team.

When Dash had his attention focused on Ember, I leaned close to Reese and quietly asked, "Have you been avoiding me for the last few weeks?"

She leaned back and said, "Of course not. Why would you even think that?" She was lying and doing a very poor job of it.

"So that's how you're going to play this? Act like nothing happened between us?" I asked, getting more pissed by the second.

She scoffed and said in a low voice, "You're the one who ran out while I was still sleeping. I figured you wanted to act like nothing happened, so that's what I've been doing. Really, Duke, we fucked, it was fun, and that's it."

I didn't care for the nonchalance in her tone, but there was something else in her statement that needed to be addressed first. "I didn't run out while you were sleeping. I had to be at work early that morning, and I didn't want to wake you. I left you a note explaining all that and telling you that I would be back when I got off work."

Her eyes widened in disbelief, then they flashed with anger. "Bullshit."

"Not bullshit. I put it on your nightstand," I insisted.

"Say whatever you want. I don't believe you. I never saw a note. Now, I'm finished discussing this with you," she snapped. Then, she took her friend by the arm and strolled off down the hall, leaving me sitting there like a fool.

Five days passed before I got a chance to talk to her again. She was a master at hiding from me. She either stayed in the room with Ember, or she was holed up in Carbon's room, neither of which I could enter freely. This time, I found her in the pool coaxing Ember to get in. When she finally did jump in, she came up with her tit hanging out of her top and ran off. Like a good friend, Reese ran after her.

Assuming I missed any small chance I had of talking to her, I dove into the pool and started swimming laps. I came to an abrupt stop when I felt a smooth hand glide from the top of my shoulder down to the small of my back. I shook the water from my hair and wiped the water from my eyes. I opened them to find Reese in her skimpy bikini standing in front of me. I didn't say a word, just stared and waited.

She looked down and very quietly said, "I found the note under my bed. It must have fallen off the nightstand or something. So, uh, sorry for being bitchy about that."

Her apology caught me off guard, and I wasn't sure how to respond. I wanted her, but I didn't want to put myself out there any more than I already had. I shrugged and held out my hand, "No worries. Friends?"

She put her hand in mine and smiled, "Friends."

We spent the rest of the day hanging out in the pool with Dash and Ember. Well, I should say that I spent the rest of the day in the pool. I couldn't get my dick to behave, and it was easier to hide my ever-present erection in the water.

When Ember decided she was ready to go back to the room, Dash quickly volunteered to walk her back, leaving Reese and I alone for the first time since the night of her prom. I placed my arms on the side of the pool and locked eyes with Reese. "Get in."

She slowly rose from the chair and strutted, yes strutted, her sexy ass the long way around the pool before she entered the water at a snail's pace. She was killing me. She waded through the water and stopped in front of me with a smirk on her face. "See something you like?"

I growled and grabbed her around her waist, pulling her body flush with mine, "You know I do." I couldn't take it any longer. I captured her lips with mine and kissed her softly, tentatively. She didn't respond immediately, but I didn't let up. After a few seconds, she slid her arms around my neck and melted into me. "Sugar," I breathed against her lips. "You've had me so hard all damn day." I pressed my hard-on against her stomach to prove my point, eliciting a groan from her.

"Is that so?" she panted, pressing herself closer to me.

Kissing my way to her earlobe, I pressed my lips to the shell of her ear and answered, "Fuck, yes."

I wasn't interested in talking anymore. Before she could protest, I pulled the strings on her top and had one tit in my mouth while my hand came up to caress the other.

She moaned and yanked on my hair. "Duke, we can't do this." The fuck we couldn't. "Not out here. Someone will see us."

With my mouth still attached to her chest, I moved us to the far corner of the pool and covered her with my body. "No one will see us over here."

"Duke," she pleaded.

"Yes or no, Reese?" Please don't say no. Please don't say no.

"Yes," she moaned.

I reached for my beer and plucked a condom from the pocket on the koozie.

"What the hell, Duke? Were you planning this?" Reese asked, clearly pissed.

For a split second, I had no idea what she meant. "Oh, shit. You haven't seen these yet?" I asked, pointing to the koozie. She shook her head and crossed her arms over her chest. "Phoenix ordered these a few months ago. It was some kind of promotion from a new company.

Anyway, all the new koozies have a pocket with a condom in it."

"Oh, well, I guess that's good," she said, stumbling over her words.

I moved closer to her, hoping like hell the damn koozie hadn't killed the mood. Running my nose along her jawline, I murmured against her neck, "I didn't plan on anything happening. Not gonna lie and say I wasn't hoping something would."

Gently nipping her neck with my teeth, I asked against her skin, "You gonna let me fuck you?"

"Please," she begged.

I hoisted my ass out of the pool, shoved my trunks out of the way, rolled the condom on, and was back in front of her in mere seconds.

"You gonna be able to stay quiet while you're taking my cock?" I asked as I moved her bathing suit bottoms to the side. I lined myself up at her entrance and waited for her answer. "Well?"

She swallowed and nodded, "I'll try."

With that, I buried myself to the hilt in one fluid thrust and covered her mouth with mine, to muffle her sounds as much as mine. Damn, her pussy was tight, warm, and the place my dick wanted to call home for the rest of his working life.

I started out slow, but that only lasted for a few thrusts. I was so worked up from watching her all day and wanting her for weeks, I was having a hard time controlling myself. I wanted to draw it out for as long as I could in case I had to wait another two weeks before I could have her again, but she felt too damn good. As it was, it would be a miracle if I lasted long enough to make sure she got off. "Reese," I gritted out, "I need you to come."

As if she was waiting for my demand, I felt her pussy start to spasm around my cock the moment the words left my mouth. Then, she clamped down on me like a fucking vice, so tight I almost couldn't move.

I slapped my hand over her mouth and bit down on her shoulder while her orgasm took over and pulled me right along with her.

I pulled back and met her eyes while I tried to catch my breath. She was so fucking beautiful, inside and out. Everything about her sucked me in and tried to consume me. It was a feeling that was unfamiliar to me, and I wasn't sure how I felt about it.

Before I could give it much thought, the back door swung open. "Duke, you out here?" Shaker called.

I quickly pulled out of Reese, tucked my condom clad dick back into my trunks, and turned around to hide her body behind mine. Propping my arms on the edge of the pool, I answered, "Yeah, man, what's up?"

"Heading to Cedar Valley to cunt hunt. You wanna ride?"

I felt Reese tense behind me. Fucking Shaker. "Nah, brother, not tonight. I'm beat," I replied honestly.

"All right, catch ya later." With that, he was gone.

As soon as the door closed, Reese was pushing against my back. "Move, Duke," she growled.

Turning back to face her, I placed my hands on her waist and frowned at the scowl on her face. "Hey, what's wrong?"

"Seriously?" she screeched. "He asked you to go on a cunt hunt not even 10 seconds after you had your dick in me!"

"Keep your voice down unless you want someone else to come out here," I warned. "He didn't know I was out here fucking you in the pool."

"And that makes it okay?"

"Who else was he going to ask? Dash is following Ember around like a lost puppy,

Phoenix and Badger never go, Carbon is MIA most weekends, Byte prefers the club whores, and the rest of the guys are either too old or too young to go."

"Move," she growled. I didn't.

"What exactly are you upset about? I told him I didn't want to go." I could understand her being upset if I had agreed to go with him, but I didn't hesitate to tell him no.

"How often do you say yes?"

"Aw, sugar, are you jealous?" I chuckled, trying to lighten the mood.

The hard shove against my chest was unexpected, causing me to take a few steps back. She climbed out of the pool, grabbed her towel, and headed for the door. "Fuck off, Duke," she said over her shoulder before she disappeared inside.

By the time I made it back inside, she was nowhere to be found.

CHAPTER THREE

Reese

It had been three days since the evening Duke and I spent by the pool. We had seen each other several times since then, but we hadn't had any time together alone. I was beginning to get frustrated with the whole situation. I knew Ember had a lot going on and needed me, but I didn't think 30 minutes or an hour to myself was asking a whole lot.

I was feeling emotional, and I didn't like it. What made it even worse was that I had no idea why I was feeling so emotional. Regardless, I did what I always did in times like that, I shut down. I started snapping at Ember. I knew I would feel bad about it later, but I couldn't care less at the time. She kept going on and on about the common room being empty while I did my best to ignore her. Finally, she got up and walked down the hall. I took the opportunity for what it was and went to my brother's room. I knocked on the door and waited.

"What?" Carbon grunted.

"Can I come in?" I hesitantly asked. If he was in there fucking some club whore, I didn't want to see it, hear it, or even know about it.

The door flew open and there stood my hulking brother. "What's wrong?"

"Nothing," I said as I brushed past him and entered his room. A quick sweep of the room revealed it was currently a whore-free zone. "I just felt like hanging out with my big scary brother. Is that okay?"

"Cut the bullshit, Reesie. What's really going on?" Carbon knew me better than anyone and could always tell when something was wrong with me. I had a love-hate relationship with that fact.

I sighed and let my shoulders slump forward, "I don't know, Carbon, honestly. I just feel like something is wrong, and I feel like crying, but I have no idea why."

He closed his door and sat down beside me on

the bed. Wrapping his arm around my shoulders, he pulled so that I was leaning into his chest. Blowing out a heavy breath, he said, "We can't find Duke."

My head shot up so fast the top of it slammed into Carbon's chin. "Fuck," he cursed while I shrieked, "What do you mean you can't find Duke?"

Carbon studied me briefly before answering, "Just what I said. We can't find him. He's not answering his phone, and no one's seen him all day." He paused and watched me, scrutinizing my every move. "When was the last time you saw him?"

Crap. Carbon was very good at reading body language, especially people he knew well. I would bet money my reactions had prompted him to suspect something was going on between me and Duke. I forced my muscles to relax and prayed my voice would cooperate when I answered, "Yesterday, in the common room at dinner. Him and Dash ate with me and Ember. I think something is going on between Dash and Ember." I was hoping to redirect his suspicions to Dash and Ember instead of me and Duke.

"The boys are out looking for him now. I'm sure it's..." he trailed off and didn't finish the lie. Carbon was a wonderful brother. After we lost our family, we became very close. He made a valiant effort to never lie to me, which is why he stopped mid-sentence. He wasn't sure it was nothing. None of them were. They were worried about him and that's why they rode out to look for him.

Suddenly, overcome with worry and dread, I burst into tears. Carbon pulled me into his chest and held me while I cried all over him. He was the one person I felt comfortable showing my emotions to. He rubbed circles on my back and murmured words of comfort to me, but nothing helped to ease my fears. In my mind, I was 11 years old again, and he'd just told me that our entire family had been murdered.

I must have fallen asleep during my crying fit because I woke to Carbon shaking me and calling my name. When I opened my eyes, I could tell by the look on his face that he was about to deliver bad news. "They found him?" I croaked.

He nodded and quickly said, "He's alive. He's hurt, but he's alive."

Feeling a little better after hearing that, I pushed myself to a sitting position and asked, "What happened?"

He shook his head and looked down at his lap,

"I don't know, Reesie. His sister called Phoenix just a little while ago. She said the hospital called to tell her Duke was there and going into emergency surgery. She wanted Phoenix and Dash to take her to the hospital. She asked that everyone else hang back until they know more. As of right now, that's all I can tell you."

I flopped back onto the bed and covered my eyes. I tried my best to hold in my sobs, but my efforts were futile. Carbon stayed by my side, running his hand over my hair, while I once again cried myself to sleep.

The next time I woke, it was to a feeling I was very familiar with. I threw the covers off of me and bolted for the bathroom. I came to a sliding stop and dropped to my knees right as the vomit broke through the tight seal of my lips.

Carbon was there seconds later, holding my hair. "Are you okay, Reesie?"

I wiped my mouth with some toilet paper and held up one finger. I wasn't sure if I was finished, and I had learned the hard way that talking too soon after puking could result in more puking, at least for me anyway. When I was sure I was done, I answered, "Yeah, I think so. You know how my stomach gets when I'm upset." That was very true. I had a "nervous stomach," which

I knew wasn't technically a real thing, but for me, every time my anxiety got out of control, I would find myself hugging a toilet bowl until the anxiety had passed.

"Do you want me to ask Patch to come see you? Maybe get you something for your stomach?" he asked, his big green eyes filled with worry.

I shook my head, "No, I don't want to take anything if I don't have to. Would you bring me a piece of toast and maybe a ginger ale? I think that will help."

"Of course."

My stomach did feel better after the toast and ginger ale, but my emotional state was much the same, if not worse. I stayed in Carbon's room and spent most of my time staring at the wall. I'm not sure how much time had passed, but finally, Carbon came in with news about Duke.

"Reesie, I'm not going to sugarcoat it. It's bad. He was stabbed eight times and suffered a severe head injury. I don't know the details of how that happened, so don't ask. What I can tell you is that he is currently in a medically induced coma and being monitored closely in the ICU. Only immediate family can visit with him right now, but we can go see him when he is moved to a room."

fight off whoever did this to him. His face was so swollen, I doubted he could have opened his eyes if he was awake. His head was shaved on one side with a thick bandage in the middle of the shaved area. I dropped my head down and let a few tears escape. I squeezed his hand and whispered, "Duke, please be okay."

When I had my emotions locked down again, I took a step back from the bed and turned to see who else was in the room. To my surprise, the only other visitors were Phoenix and a woman I assumed to be Duke's sister.

"Reese, this is Harper, Duke's sister. Harper, this is Reese, Carbon's sister," Phoenix said.

The automated response spilled from my lips, "Hi, Harper. I'm so sorry about your brother. Is there anything I can do to help?" I was sorry about Duke, but I didn't really want to do anything to help her. If I had been in a better place emotionally, I would have been more than willing to offer my help, but as it was, I was in no shape to take on any burdens.

"Actually, there is something you could do for me. Phoenix said you might be willing to stay with Duke while I go get a shower and a few hours of sleep. I'm exhausted, and I stink, but I don't want him to wake up with no one here.

Would that be okay?" she asked.

Well, fuck me sideways. What had I gotten myself into? "That's fine with me as long as it's okay with Phoenix," I said, turning my gaze to Phoenix.

Please say I can't stay.

Please say I can't stay.

"That's fine, just make sure you stay in the room. You can ride back to the clubhouse with whoever brings Harper back," he said, clearly not hearing my unspoken plea. "I'm going to walk Harper down, and then I have a few errands to run."

Next thing I knew, I was alone with Duke. I guess the saying "Be careful what you wish for" was true. I had repeatedly wished to have some time alone with Duke, and now I did. Fucking great.

CHAPTER FOUR

Duke

My mind seemed to wake up before my body did. Everything hurt and nothing worked. No matter what I did, I couldn't get my eyes to open. I couldn't get any of my body parts to voluntarily move, and I couldn't make a sound. For a brief moment, I thought I might be dead, but then I remembered the pain. What in the hell was going on?

I tried to quiet my mind and pay attention to what I could hear. At least my ears seemed to be working. There was a rhythmic beeping and the sounds of some kind of cloth or clothing being rustled. A door opened and closed, and then I heard footsteps. I felt a hand touch mine, and then I heard her voice. Reese.

"Duke, please wake up. It's been days. Days! I need you to wake up. I can't handle this. It's too much for me. Everything is too much. I need you. I need you to wake up. Please," she said and sniffled. Was she crying? Reese didn't cry. Before I could figure out what was going on or where we were, I drifted off into the black abyss again.

The next time I woke, I heard Reese's voice right away. "I have to go back to the clubhouse when your sister gets here. Please, Duke, please come back to us. Please." I felt something wet land on my nose, and then her lips ever so gently touched my cheek.

Off and on I woke, hearing a variety of voices and conversations each time. Every time I woke, I tried with everything I had to move or make some kind of noise, but nothing worked. I would try and try until I fell back into the black.

One of the last times I woke in my paralyzed like state, I heard Reese's voice again. She was talking to someone. I soon realized the other voice belonged to my sister. "Reese, honey, are you sure you're okay? You've been in that bathroom throwing up every day for the last week. If you're sick, you really shouldn't be around Duke."

"I'm not sick, Harper. I already told you. My stomach gets upset like this when I'm worried or stressed. Trust me, it's not contagious," Reese snapped back.

Harper huffed, "This is none of my business, but are you pregnant?"

I heard Reese gasp and quickly answer, "Of course I'm not pregnant. It's not even a possibility." It was a possibility; she and I both knew that. Condoms weren't one hundred percent effective. I assumed she was on birth control, as most girls her age were, but that wasn't one hundred percent effective either. Even though the chance was small, it was still a possibility. And by the way Reese answered, I would guess it was a certainty.

The next conversation I recalled hearing was a one-sided conversation Reese was having. I assumed she was on the phone since I couldn't hear the other person. "I'm sure. I don't want it. It's not up to him, it's my decision to make. I don't care about the money. I just want it gone as fast as possible. Just set it up, and let me know the time and place. I'll be there."

Not long after that, Harper arrived to relieve Reese. I'm guessing they had been tag teaming staying with me so that I was never left alone in the hospital. "I hope your appointment goes well. Will you be back this afternoon?" Harper asked.

"Thanks. I'm not sure if I'll be back or not. It depends on how long it takes. I'll call and let you know," Reese replied.

So, she was pregnant with my child and she was off to have an abortion while I was laid up in the fucking hospital unable to have any say in what she was doing. By the time she got back, awake or not, it would already be done, and there would be nothing I could do about it. Consumed with fury, I gladly let the blackness take me away.

The next time my mind came back online, I did the same thing I did each time before. I tried to open my eyes first. They opened. Holy shit, my eyes opened! My vision was blurry, but it was steadily clearing. The next thing I tried was my voice. It worked. I made some unintelligible sound, but it was enough. Harper's face was directly in front of mine seconds later.

She yelled my name as tears fell from her eyes. I winced from the sheer volume of her voice. "Tone it down would you, sis? My fucking head is killing me."

"That's because you had brain surgery. And excuse me for being happy. You've been in a coma for a week and a half," she snapped.

What? A week and a half? That couldn't be right. "You're shitting me, right?"

"I most certainly am not. It's been the longest 10 days of my life. I didn't know if you would ever come out of it, and they couldn't even tell us if you would be the same if you did wake up. Clearly, you're the same asshole you were before your attack."

"My attack?" I asked.

"You don't remember?" she asked. I shook my head. "You were attacked by someone or someones. You were stabbed eight times and had a severe head injury. Any of that ring a bell?"

It didn't. I remembered leaving the clubhouse and riding into town. The last thing I could remember was riding down Main Street. After that, nothing. I was lost in my thoughts, trying desperately to remember what in the hell happened to me when a nurse and two doctors entered the room.

"Mr. Jackson, good to see you awake. How are you feeling?" the man I assumed to be a doctor asked.

The next portion of the day was spent being examined by two different physicians, answering a litany of questions, and going through a series of ridiculous medical tests. By the time they were finished, I was exhausted, which of course is when Phoenix showed up. I did my best to answer his questions and then played the I'm too tired for any more right now card.

Truth be told, I wanted to see Reese. We apparently had some things to discuss, but it's not like I could ask for her. I would just have to wait until she showed up in my room. Unfortunately for me, that didn't happen until two days later. By that time, I was well and truly pissed.

I was pretending to be asleep when Reese walked in. I maintained the façade until I was sure that my sister had left. Then, I opened my eyes and waited for her to notice me. It didn't take long. She smiled and came closer to the bed. "Duke, I'm so glad you're awake. I've been so worried about you."

I just stared at her. During the time I had to brood, I decided that I would give her a dose of her own medicine. In other words, I was going to shut down and not talk. Immature? Absolutely. Did I care? Not one bit. Eventually, she stopped trying to talk to me and returned to her seat. This pattern continued for several days before she stopped coming to the hospital altogether.

Then, one day, she showed up out of the blue. I called and asked one of my brothers to bring me my laptop and a few other necessities. According to Reese, no one other than her was available to bring the requested items to me. She assured me that she was only dropping off the items and had no plans to stay. That was until she received a text message. She held up her phone and showed me the text.

Carbon: Stay in Duke's room and don't leave for any reason. Not until you hear from me and only me. Life or death, Reesie. Love you.

I nodded and turned away from her. I didn't have a choice. I had to let her stay, but that didn't mean I had to talk to her. I maintained my silence for hours. Finally, her phone buzzed again, and she let out a sigh. When she started gathering her things, I asked, "Going somewhere?"

She whirled around, eyes wide. "Yes, I'm leaving. Carbon just sent a text telling me to meet him downstairs."

"Good," I said harshly. "Be sure you don't come back."

"What is your problem, Duke?" she asked.

I unleashed all the pent-up anger that had stewed for days. I said things just to hurt her, to get her to leave and not come back. I was angry about so many different things, and I took every single one of them out on her. I expected her to lash out, to yell at me, or to at least show some kind of reaction, but no, not Reese Walker. She waited until I finished my tirade, picked up her belongings, and walked out the door. Little did I know, she was also walking out of my life.

CHAPTER FIVE

Duke

One year later

"Good job today, Noel!" I said to the little girl at my side.

"Thanks, Mr. Duke. That was my first time jumping. Did you see me?" Noel asked excitedly.

"I sure did. You're going to know more about horses than me pretty soon. Are you going to quit school and start working here?"

She giggled, "My mom would never let me do that."

I patted her head. "Good, because school is important. I'll finish up with Buttercup for you.

See you next week."

"Thank you! Bye, Mr. Duke." She ran off to find her mother while I untacked the horse. I finished grooming her and led her back to her stall. Buttercup was a sweet horse, and Noel was an even sweeter little girl. Each of her siblings had a horse boarded at Blackwings Stables, but Noel and Buttercup were by far my favorite.

Ring! Ring!

I pulled my phone from my pocket and looked at the screen. I didn't recognize the number, but it was a Devil Springs area code, so I figured it was Copper or one of his guys. "Yeah," I answered.

The nasally voice of a middle-aged, and I would guess snobby, woman filled my ear. "Could I please speak with Mr. Jackson?"

"Speaking."

"Hi, Mr. Jackson, this is Rita from Sunshine Springs Daycare. James's mother hasn't picked him up and we can't get in touch with her—"

I interrupted, "I'm sorry, I think you have the wrong person."

She huffed, "Is this Mr. John Wayne Jackson?" At the sound of my full name, I was suddenly on edge.

"Well, yes."

"Good. We can't get in touch with Reese, so we

need you to come pick up your son."

Pick up my what?

Reese?

James?

My heart felt like it was going to beat out of my chest. My lungs refused to move air as realization dawned, and a feeling of dread washed over me.

"Mr. Jackson? Are you still there?"

"Um, uh, I'm two hours away." Yes, that was all I could come up with. My son? My freaking son? I had a son? And where the hell was Reese?

"We closed 30 minutes ago. If someone isn't here to pick him up within the next 30 minutes, we will have to notify the police and child services."

"No. No, don't do that. I have family that lives there. I'll have my cousin come pick him up. His name is Judge, I mean Jonah Jackson."

"Please inform him of the time constraints. Reese has always been on time or early to get him, and James is such a sweet boy, but I'm bound by policy, you understand?"

"Yes, fine. I need to go so I can call him and get him there in time. Thank you, Rita." I hung up before she could say anything else.

With shaking hands, I quickly dialed Judge, praying he picked up.

"Sup, cuz?"

"Judge, I need you to get a cage and get your ass to Sunshine Springs Daycare before 7:00 pm," I barked into the phone.

"Why? What the hell are you talking about?"

"Apparently, they are closed, and my fucking son hasn't been picked up today!" I bellowed.

At that, he didn't ask any more questions. I was grateful because I didn't have any answers. "I'm leaving now. I'll call you when I have him. I assume you're headed this way?"

"Damn right I am. Be there soon. Thanks, man."

Fifteen minutes later I was flying down the highway on my bike when Judge texted to let me know he had my son in his care. I didn't stop to reply to him. He knew I was on my way and couldn't respond.

The drive to Devil Springs was the longest drive of my life. I had a son. A son I knew nothing about other than his name, which I just learned. Fuck, I didn't even know his last name.

Why didn't Reese tell me about him? Why would she do this to me? Better yet, where in the hell was she? The more I thought about it, the more uneasy I became. Reese wasn't the kind of woman to abandon a baby. The daycare lady even said Reese always picked him up early or on time. Had something happened to her? Was she okay?

I needed to call Carbon. Fuck, Carbon! He knew I had a kid and didn't tell me. I was going to kick his big, burly ass when I saw him next. Phoenix could say or do whatever he wanted, but as far as I was concerned, Carbon was no longer my brother. We stood behind each other, put the club first, always, and that included his little sister. Damn him!

When I pulled through the gates at the Devil Springs clubhouse, I was still angry, and worried, and nervous. I was about to see my son for the first time, to hold him, to care for him. How was I going to care for him? I knew nothing about babies, which didn't really matter because I didn't have any of the shit babies needed. Sweat popped up on my forehead, and my vision started to blur. I couldn't do this. I couldn't take care of a baby.

A warm, very large hand landed on my shoulder and gently shook me. "Take a deep breath, brother, and come inside," Copper said.

My voice came out almost as a whisper, "I don't know if I can."

"You can, and you will. Your son is in there,

and he needs you. Now go," he ordered. God bless Copper. I needed that. I don't think I could have gone inside otherwise.

I walked into the common room, which was almost an exact replica of the Croftridge common room. In the far corner of the room, Judge was seated on a sofa with a little blue bundle in his arms. My steps halted at the sight, until Copper's big hand shoved me forward.

I slowly approached the sofa. I couldn't make myself meet anyone's eyes. I was scared. I was a big, badass biker, and I was terrified of a tiny baby. My baby. I was on the verge of turning around and running out the door when Judge spoke, "Hey, lil' man, your daddy's here." Fuck me.

I quickened my steps and dropped down beside Judge. He straightened and leaned forward, placing the blue bundle in my arms. I heard coos and giggles as I slowly reached to push the blanket away so I could see his face. I gasped and felt tears prick the backs of my eyes when I saw him for the first time. He was a perfect combination of me and Reese. He took my breath away. I couldn't speak. All I could do was stare at the perfection squirming in my arms.

Judge clapped me on the shoulder, "You all right, man?"

I cleared my throat, but didn't bother to wipe away the one tear that slid down my face, "Yeah, I think so." Then, the panic came back with a vengeance. My eyes widened, fear filling them, "I don't know what to do with a baby. I don't know how to take care of him. I don't have any of the shit he needs. I don't—"

"Calm down, Duke," Judge said. "I called my mom. She's on her way now. I have a cage and a car seat for him. He had a diaper bag and some shit at the daycare. It'll be okay."

My mind was not functioning at full capacity. I couldn't focus on anything but James. "Thanks, man."

Copper had been standing to the side, silently watching the show. He stepped forward and addressed me, "Where is his mother?"

My head shot up, "That's a good fucking question!"

Copper put his hands up, "Calm down, Duke. I'm not accusing you of anything. I'm just trying to get an idea of what's happening here."

"What's happening here is that bitch had my baby and didn't bother to fucking tell me he existed, yet she had the audacity to list me as the emergency contact at the daycare. Today, she decided not to show up to get him, and he damn near ended up with child services!" I roared.

"And who is this bitch?" Copper asked the million dollar question.

I growled, "Reese Walker."

Copper rubbed his chin with his thumb and forefinger, "That doesn't sound like Reesie Piecie."

Suddenly, something occurred to me. "Wait a minute. I thought you were keeping an eye on her. How the fuck could you not tell me about my son?" I yelled, causing the baby to cry.

"Duke!" My Aunt Leigh, Judge's mom, scolded when she heard us yelling and the baby crying. When did she arrive? She plucked the baby from my arms, grabbed the diaper bag from the floor, and announced, "We'll just be down the hall so you boys can finish sorting things out."

"I'll let that one slide, but you watch your tone. You're in my clubhouse, and you will show me respect. Now, before you go digging a hole you can't climb out of, I didn't know about the baby. None of us did. We did watch her, but we couldn't ever get close to her."

"You couldn't tell she was pregnant? You didn't see the freaking baby?" I questioned. This shit was unbelievable.

"I know it sounds crazy, but we had no idea she was pregnant, and we never saw the baby. She must have known we were checking up on her. She always parked in the garage and closed the door before she got out. She's got tint on her windows, so we couldn't see anything in the back seat," he explained.

I couldn't think of a damn thing to say. I looked at the ground and pinched the bridge of my nose. I could feel a headache coming on. Ever since my attack, I would get severe headaches from time to time. My doctor said they were likely brought on by stress. Guess he was right.

Copper pulled his phone from his pocket. "Excuse me," he said, before disappearing down a hallway.

"Did you talk to anybody before you left? Carbon or Phoenix?" Judge asked.

"No, and fuck Carbon. You guys may not have known, but there is no way she managed to keep that shit from Carbon," I spat. My anger was ramping up, which meant my head was pounding harder.

"Don't jump to conclusions. Carbon hasn't been back to Devil Springs since he left with Reese after their family was murdered. When they came back, she went to live with their grandmother, and he moved to Croftridge with Phoenix and the rest of you."

"Bullshit. You guys have had our club up here for parties many times since then."

"Yeah, but think back, Carbon didn't come to a single one. He would go visit Reese and their grandmother in Reedy Fork whenever we had a party. Reese missing is probably the only thing that could get him to come back here, and I have a bad feeling that we're about to test that theory," Judge said.

"You really think she's missing?" I asked. I wasn't sure that I believed that yet. Or, maybe I didn't want to believe it.

I didn't notice that Copper had returned until he chimed in, "I tried to call her, but her phone is going straight to voicemail. I sent Batta and Tiny to ride out to her house and see if she was there or if anything seemed out of place. I checked with her boss, and she did show up at work today. Said she didn't notice anything out of the ordinary, but Reese did ask if she could leave an hour early."

I dropped down to the sofa. I was exhausted and my head was not letting up. I needed to at least get off of my feet for a bit. "You'll have to excuse me; my circuits are overloaded at the moment. What exactly are you getting at?"

"I think something happened to Reese between when she got off work and when you received the call from the daycare. Spazz, see if you can get into her phone records, maybe get a location. We need to call Carbon and Phoenix. Duke, it's your choice. I'll be happy to make that call for you."

"Thanks, Copper, but I think I should be the one to call Carbon. He's going to lose his shit, so if you could wait a few minutes and then give Phoenix a call, that would be helpful."

"No problem. You can go in my office if you want some privacy," he offered.

I sat down in his office and took in a deep breath. I did not want to make this call. I raised the phone to my ear and waited.

"Duke, what's happenin', brother?" Carbon answered.

I cleared my throat, "Carbon, man, um, I don't know how to tell you this, so I'm just going to say it. I was called to Devil Springs today to pick up my son from daycare because his mother didn't show up to get him. I think something has happened to Reese."

I was met with a few beats of silence before he exploded. "WHAT? What the fuck, Duke?

Your son? My sister? You better be fucking with me. I'm gonna kick your ass either way, but you better not be speaking the truth to me right now!!" he roared.

Well, he took that about as well as I expected. "Look, I didn't know about him until today. So, be pissed, flip your shit, whatever. Just get your ass up here!"

He didn't say anything. I could hear him breathing, heavily, but he remained silent. Finally, he choked out, "I can't," and then the line went dead.

Copper entered his office with his phone to his ear. "Yeah, he's right here, hang on." He handed his phone to me, "It's Phoenix."

"Prez," I mumbled into the phone.

"Duke, brother, we're heading out now and Carbon will be coming with us, willingly or not. Hang in there, brother."

I handed the phone back to Copper, completely confused by Phoenix's reaction. He didn't sound pissed at all. He sounded like he understood. Hell, I guess he did. He knew what it was like to find out you had a kid you knew nothing about. He also knew what it was like for your woman to be missing, not that Reese was my woman. She wasn't, but she was my child's mother.

Oh, who was I kidding? I wanted Reese from the moment I met her, and I still did.

Shit.

CHAPTER SIX

Duke

"Phoenix and some of his crew are about 45 minutes out, but go ahead and tell us what you found," Copper said to Batta and Tiny. They had just returned from Reese's house.

"We didn't see any signs of a struggle or forced entry. Everything was locked up tight when we arrived. Her car wasn't there, neither was she. We did find some letters in her bedroom that we thought might be of interest," Batta said. Tiny handed a small stack of papers to Copper.

Copper scanned the page on top, growled, flipped to the next one, growled louder, and then rapidly flipped through all of the papers. "What the fuck is this shit?"

I snatched the papers from Copper and flipped through them myself. I couldn't believe what I was seeing. "Why wouldn't she tell anyone she was receiving threats?" I wondered out loud.

"Do we have any idea when she got these? Is there a possibility that these are old?" Copper asked no one in particular.

Judge chimed in, "I think it's safe to assume those are recent given the fact that she is currently missing." I knew that; I just didn't want to acknowledge it. I was certain Carbon knew nothing about the threats. He wouldn't have left her up here alone if he had.

Shit.

Shit.

Shit.

"Spazz, any luck with her phone?" Bronze asked.

"Not a damn thing. The last time she used it was yesterday. Don't know if the battery is dead or what, but I can't get a location on it," Spazz told us, dejectedly.

"All right, Tiny, round up about five guys and the prospects. Spread out through town and see if you can spot her or her car anywhere," Copper ordered.

The clubhouse doors crashed open revealing a furious and frantic Carbon. Phoenix stood just behind him, looking like he was going to strangle Carbon. What the hell? I thought they were still at least 30 minutes away.

"Update! Now!" Carbon roared. He looked like a rabid beast with his wild eyes and his chest heaving.

Phoenix clapped his hand on Carbon's shoulder and squeezed. "Lock it down, brother, or I'll be locking you down, feel me?" he warned. Phoenix was the only one close to Carbon's intimidating size and had the best shot at controlling him if he went on a rampage.

Carbon's nostrils flared, his chest rose and fell with his heavy breaths. He nodded, but didn't say anything else. He fixed his eyes on Copper and waited for him to speak.

Copper promptly filled them in on what we knew so far and handed the letters to Carbon. He looked at the papers, one by one. Then, the big guy dropped to his knees and hung his head. The sound that erupted from him could only be described as the pained cry of a wounded animal. I knew this was hard for him, being in the town where his family was killed, and now his only living sibling was missing.

We gave him a moment to pull himself together. He quieted, but remained hunched over. Copper carefully asked, "We know you didn't know about the threats, but do you have any idea as to who may have sent them?"

Carbon shook his head. "No idea, Copper." He hung his head again. "My baby sister was up here dealing with so much on her own, and I had no idea because I was too much of a pussy to come back to this town. Damn. It!"

Phoenix, being the only one who could get away with speaking to Carbon in such a way, ordered, "Not now, Carbon. Get your ass off the floor and get it into gear. Reese needs you. Man up for your sister."

I wouldn't have believed it if I hadn't seen it for myself. All emotion disappeared from Carbon's face. He rose from the floor in one fluid motion, straightened his spine, squared his shoulders, and nodded. Carbon the frightened brother was gone, and the stone-cold enforcer had returned.

We heard the rumble of several Harleys approaching the forecourt. By the sound of it, the rest of the Croftridge crew had arrived. Moments later, Badger, Dash, Byte, Shaker, Edge, and Prospect Coal entered the common room. Surprisingly, it was Byte who spoke first.

"Did you get a location on her phone? What about her car?"

"Spazz couldn't locate her phone," I answered. "Some of the Devil Springs brothers rode out a bit ago to see if they could spot her car."

Byte scoffed and plopped down at a nearby table. He pulled his laptop out of his backpack and started clicking keys. "I need her cell phone number and make and model of her car, license plate if you have it."

Copper gave him the information he requested, even the license plate, which surprised me. He shrugged, "We only ever saw her in her car and I have a photographic memory."

Byte continued clicking, "Fuck! I'm getting nothing on her phone."

More clicking.

"Fuck yeah! Got her car!" he shouted.

Carbon pounced like a starving dog, "Where?"

"I sent you the coordinates," he said as Carbon's phone dinged.

"I'm going with you," I informed him. He didn't respond as he walked out the door.

Phoenix ordered, "Edge and Coal, follow them with the cage." I wish I didn't hear his next words, which I assumed were directed at Copper, but I did. "You got a doc in the club or someone you use when you need to be patched up?" I'm guessing Copper nodded because Phoenix continued speaking, "Good. Get them here now, just in case."

CHAPTER SEVEN

Duke

Carbon looked at the coordinates and knew exactly where her car was. He was on his bike and out of the parking lot in mere seconds. It was all I could do to keep up with him. That fucker was fast for a big guy.

It didn't take us long to get there. I was surprised we both made it in one piece and also that we didn't get picked up by the local police. I had never driven so fast and so recklessly on unfamiliar roads before, but we had to get to her as fast as possible. I just knew something was wrong, I could feel it in my gut.

We stopped on the side of a dark, winding

mountain road. The tire marks on the pavement and the mangled guardrail indicated we were likely in the right spot. Walking closer to the guardrail, I studied the surrounding area. Brush and small trees leading to a drop-off had been flattened, and tire tracks were clearly visible, right up to the edge.

I looked toward Carbon. He was frozen in place, just like I was. Neither of us said a word. If we didn't say it, maybe it wasn't true. But we both knew what happened.

Her car went over, and there was no way she could have survived.

We were both still standing there in silence when Edge and Coal pulled up in the cage, followed shortly by Phoenix, Dash, and Copper. Phoenix walked up to the guardrail and looked out at the drop-off. He shook his head and turned back to me, "Did she...?"

I could barely speak; it was almost a whisper, "Looks that way."

Phoenix nodded solemnly. He walked over to Edge and Coal and whispered something to them. He walked back to where I was standing and quietly said, "I'm going to need you and Copper to help me get Carbon in the cage. I can tell by just looking at him that he's going to lose it any second now. Can't say I blame him, but it's going to take all three of us and even that might not be enough."

"Now?" I asked.

"Yeah. The sooner the better."

Phoenix carefully approached Carbon first and placed his hand on his shoulder. I started moving quickly toward them, expecting Carbon to respond with violence. Shockingly, the big man crumpled to the ground in the middle of the road and roared his pain into the night. He folded in on himself, his body shaking as he sobbed. We all stood there quietly, giving him our silent support. I had tears running down my own face, and I bet every brother there did as well.

In between Carbon's cries of pain, I heard it. I wasn't sure at first, but then I heard it again. "Shhh!" I hissed. "Did you hear that?"

"No, what was it?" Dash asked.

"Listen," I whisper-yelled as I walked closer to the edge of the road.

"Help me." It wasn't loud, but it was definitely a female calling for help.

I whirled around. "You heard that, right?"

Obviously, they did because Carbon was on his feet and running toward the drop-off, the rest of the brothers right behind him.

"Get a flashlight!" Phoenix yelled.

"Already did, Prez," Coal said and proudly handed a flashlight to Phoenix.

Phoenix turned it on, and what we saw will forever be ingrained in my memory. There, about 20 feet down, was Reese's car, precariously sitting in a large tree, with Reese still inside. My eyes met hers, filled with a mixture of fear and relief.

Copper started barking orders, "Someone call 9-1-1! We need a couple of fire trucks out here. Check the cage and your bikes. Bring me all of the rope and cordage you can find. Hurry!"

I ran to my bike. I kept paracord in one of the storage compartments. The uses for it were endless, and it didn't take up much space, so I always kept some. I also had a few chains and tie-down straps, so I grabbed those, too.

I took the items over to Copper, where he was engaged in a heated conversation with Phoenix. "You can't be serious! I'm not letting you do this!"

"I am doing this, and you're not going to stop me. What if it was Ember in that car? You would want someone to go down there and get her. I just happen to be here and have experience with these types of rescues. We don't have time to wait for the fire department to get here. We don't have time for this bullshit either. Help me make a harness and get the ropes ready," Copper returned.

"Even if you can get down there to her, you might not be able to get her back up. What if she's hurt?" Phoenix questioned.

Copper was already working on his harness, "Take a look at that car, Phoenix. It's moving. It ain't going to stay in that tree much longer. I can hear the wood creaking as we speak. We have to get her out now. If I can't get her back up, which I damn well know I can, I'll hang there with her until the trucks get here with better equipment to pull us up."

Carbon was silently stringing rope together and quickly tying knots. Once he was finished, he looped the rope around a large tree trunk and secured it. He moved to a nearby tree trunk and repeated the process.

I watched in awe as my brothers worked as fast as they could to create a rudimentary rope rescue system from the items a few of us had on our bikes. I probably should have been watching Reese, trying to reassure her that help was on the way, but I just couldn't. I wasn't strong enough to look into those big green eyes filled with fear.

I couldn't stomach the thought of watching her plummet to her death if the car fell. I was scared and weak, and very much ashamed of myself, but that didn't change anything.

When the ropes were ready, Copper went to the edge of the drop-off, and Carbon and Phoenix began to carefully lower him. More flashlights had materialized. I could clearly see Reese, and to my horror, I could clearly see blood. I started to turn away again, unable to watch the scene before me, when she said my name, "Duke." That one word, my name, uttered as a broken sob, was filled with so much pain it almost brought me to my knees.

I locked eyes with her. She placed her hand on the window, tears running down her face, and asked, "James?" She was on the verge of death and she was worried about our son.

"He's okay," I rasped out.

Her relief was visible. Her lips trembled with her next words, "I'm so sorry."

What could I say? I wanted to yell and scream at her. How could she have kept my son from me? If she hadn't wrecked her car, how long would she have kept him from me? I couldn't do that, though. There were more important things to focus on.

69

I was still trying to formulate a response when Copper reached the car. Reese sobbed in earnest when she saw him. I'm not sure what Copper said to her, but she shook her head. He said something else, and she shook her head again. The next thing Copper said was clearly heard, "You have to, Reesie Piecie. You have to!"

She grimaced, clearly in pain, as she tried to move. She gingerly maneuvered her body and lowered the back of her seat. She looked to Copper, her face full of uncertainty. He nodded. She took in a breath and started crawling toward the back seat.

The tree creaked and groaned with the shifting of the car. Where in the hell was the fire department? If they didn't get here soon, we were going to have two casualties on our hands.

Carbon shifted his weight and leaned to one side. Dash walked in a different direction, pulling firmly on the rope he was holding, while Phoenix held his rope steady. They were moving Copper toward the rear of the car. My heart was pounding, my chest tight, but I couldn't take my eyes off of Reese.

She pulled herself through the rear window. She wasn't putting weight on her left arm, and her left foot was limply resting at an odd angle.

Carefully, she balanced herself on the trunk of her car. Carbon and Dash made adjustments with the ropes, inching Copper toward her.

The car shifted, raising Reese about a foot above Copper. Her shrill scream reverberated through the night air. Scooting herself to the edge of the trunk, she nervously looked down to Copper.

Dash, Phoenix, and Carbon were furiously pulling on the ropes, trying to raise him up. Everything was happening too fast. Before they could get Copper lifted to Reese again, the top of the tree snapped.

Reese jumped.

The car fell.

Copper caught her.

And that's when the fucking fire department finally arrived.

CHAPTER EIGHT

Duke

My Aunt Leigh walked into the emergency department waiting room carrying my sleeping baby boy, with Judge at her side. They sat down beside me, and she laid James in my arms. "How is she?"

I looked down at my son. My son. I still wasn't used to that. I gently ran my hand over his fuzzy head. "I haven't heard anything yet. Carbon went back with her and hasn't come out."

"Do you guys have any idea how the wreck happened?" Judge asked.

"I don't know if she has said anything to Carbon, but I can tell you she was hit by another car, no question about that."

"How do you know?" Judge asked.

"Her car looked like it had been T-boned. Couldn't have been damage from going over the drop-off. Edge had the foresight to take some pictures of the car when we first got there, in case it fell. Good thing he did, too. You can clearly see paint from the other car. The police are up there now looking at the tire marks and trying to reconstruct the accident."

The emergency department doors opened, and Carbon emerged. He looked directly at me. "She's asking for James," he croaked.

I stood with my son in my arms. Carbon reached for him, but I shook my head. "I'll take him back to her."

Carbon's jaw clenched. He gritted out, "You got a right to be pissed. I do, too, so I get that, but don't you dare upset her right now."

I nodded. "I won't. Just going to take my boy back to her and see for myself how she is."

It was almost a whisper from the big man, "Thank you."

Reese went into a fit of great, gulping sobs when she laid eyes on James. She reached for him with her one good arm—the other was in a cast and strapped across her with a sling. "My baby," she cried.

James woke at the sound of her voice. His eyes darted around the room to find her. When he did, he launched his little body forward, causing me to almost drop him. "Can I lay him right there?" I gestured to the space between her good arm and her body.

She nodded, tears steadily falling from her lashes. I placed him beside her, and she seemed to instantly calm. She leaned down to smell the top of his head and gave him a gentle kiss. "I love you so much, sweet boy," she murmured to him. He cooed and smiled up at her.

I cleared my throat, "Are you okay?"

She shrugged with her good shoulder. "Broken arm. Broken ankle. Staples in my head. Lots of cuts and bruises. Oh, stitches in my thigh. Probably going to have to have surgery on my ankle."

"Honestly, Reese, that's not too bad, all things considered."

Her nonchalance vanished, "You're right. I'm lucky to be alive."

"A lot of people are damn glad you are. When we first got there, we thought we'd lost you. If we hadn't heard you calling for help, we would have lost you."

She looked at me curiously, "How did you

guys find me?"

I gestured toward the chair in the corner of her room, "May I?" She nodded. I took a seat and told her everything that happened, starting with the phone call from the daycare.

She interrupted me at that part, "Duke, I'm so sorry about—"

I held up my hand to stop her. "We're not discussing that right now," then I continued telling her how we found her.

Just as I finished, there was a knock on the door. Apparently, that was just a warning because they didn't wait to enter her room. Two uniformed police officers walked in. "Reese Walker, we need to ask you some questions about the accident. Is now a good time?"

I stood to tell them to leave, but Reese stopped me. "It's fine. Duke, can you please get James for me while I talk to the officers?"

"Yes, but I'm staying in here," I firmly stated.

"That's fine. Please, officers, what can I help you with?"

"I'm Officer Bullard and this is my partner Officer Peterson. Can you tell us about the accident?"

"Sure. I left work a little earlier than usual because I needed to go by my grandmother's old house to pick up something and be back in time to pick James up from daycare. I noticed a car following me a little too closely. When the road straightened, the car passed me. I didn't think anything of it at the time, but farther down the road that very same car came out of nowhere and plowed into the side of my car." Reese stopped there and looked down at her lap. Her breath hitched, but she managed to continue, "Most people stop when they hit something, but that's not what happened. She just kept going until my car went through the guardrail and over the drop-off. I did everything I could to stop. I stood on my brakes, pulled up the emergency brake, but nothing worked."

"You said 'she.' The driver was female?" Officer Bullard asked.

"Yes."

"Can you tell us about the car? Color, make, model?"

"It was a yellow Nissan Xterra, with a brush guard on the front," Reese answered confidently.

The other officer chimed in, "When it passed you, did you happen to notice the license plate?"

"I didn't get the number, but I did notice that it was an Arizona plate."

"Good. What about the driver? Did you get a

good look at her?"

"Not really. She had dark, curly hair and was wearing large sunglasses. That's about all I could see of her."

"Do you know anyone from Arizona? Anyone who would want to hurt you?"

Reese shook her head. "Nope."

"Okay, I think that's all for now. Here's my card. Please give me a call if you think of anything else that might be helpful. For now, we'll see if we can track down the car and driver that hit you. We should have the accident report ready for your insurance company by tomorrow. Do you want us to mail you a copy or would you like to come pick it up at the station?"

I answered for her, "I'll come pick it up tomorrow."

They both looked to Reese. "That's fine, Duke can pick it up."

"All right. We'll get out of your hair. I'd go buy a lottery ticket if I were you. You were awfully lucky tonight," Officer Bullard said.

Reese smiled, "I just might do that. Thank you, officers."

I opened my mouth to speak, but Patch entered the room before I could utter a word. He was dressed in light blue scrubs covered by the standard white coat. "Reese, my dear, what happened?"

"Patch? What are you doing here?" she squeaked.

"I work here. The group I work for has us rotate through the smaller hospitals in the area, and tonight I was scheduled here. I looked to see which patient I needed to see next and saw your name on the board. What happened? Are you okay?"

"I was in a car accident. My arm and ankle are broken. I have a few cuts and bruises, but I'll heal," she said, as if she hadn't been trapped in a car mere moments from plunging to her death just a few hours ago.

"Are you in any pain right now?" he asked, his face full of genuine concern.

"I'm hurting, but it's nothing like it was when I first got here. This I can handle."

He glanced over to me, then down to the baby in my lap. He opened his mouth, but I shook my head and mouthed, "Not now, Patch."

He turned back to Reese, "You want me to see if I can get you out of here?"

"Hell, yes. I hate hospitals. No offense," she exclaimed.

"None taken, sweetheart. A lot of people feel

that way. I'll go look over your chart and talk to the doctor who saw you when you came in. Now, if everything is in order and we let you go home, you can't stay by yourself—"

I cut him off, "She'll be staying at the clubhouse tonight." He arched a brow. "Copper's clubhouse."

"I most certainly am not," she huffed.

"Okay, you tell that to your brother. Someone intentionally rammed into your car and pushed you over the side of a fucking mountain, Reese! Carbon isn't going to let you stay at your house and neither am I. It's the clubhouse, or you stay here. Pick one," I ordered.

"Fine," she said sullenly. "Clubhouse it is."

"Well, that's settled. I'll go see what I can do," Patch said and left the room.

"What the hell, Duke?" she shouted at me.

"I know about the letters, Reese." She gasped. "Don't want to talk about it now. Let's just get you somewhere safe and get some rest. It's been a rough night for all of us."

CHAPTER NINE

Reese

Carbon carried me into the clubhouse. I had crutches and could have walked, but he insisted. I knew he was having a hard time dealing with the fact that he almost lost me. After our parents and two siblings were killed, Carbon and I became very close and stayed that way until this past year. That was my fault, too. The last year of my life, well year and a half, had been nothing but a series of fuck-ups. Fuck-ups that I was going to have to explain to several people in the very near future.

Carbon placed me on a bed in one of the clubhouse bedrooms. He gently sat down beside me, and his haunted eyes found mine. "Reese," he croaked.

I reached out and pulled him into a one-armed hug. "Don't go there, big scary brother. I'm here. I'm a little hurt, but I'm still here." His shoulders shook, but he remained silent. He was killing me. My ferocious, badass brother was crying, because of me. I didn't say anything, just silently waited with my arm around him, allowing him to hide his face in my neck.

When he got his emotions under control, he pulled back and boldly informed me, "You're coming back to Croftridge. I'm not giving you a choice. I almost lost you tonight. If we'd been even a minute later getting to you, I would have lost you. If you're closer, I can get to you faster. If you're closer, I can watch over you. I've missed you, little sister, and I want you to come back home."

With watery eyes, I agreed without argument, "Okay."

I must have surprised him with my answer because he did a double take before nodding once and standing. "You want me to get your boy for you?"

"Please."

Carbon returned holding my whole world in his hands. He smiled down at James, "You named him after Dad."

"And Mason. His full name is James Mason Jackson," I said softly.

"How old is he?"

"Four months."

He nodded. "I'm not going to lie," he said, continuing to look down at my sweet boy, "I was fucking pissed as hell when Duke called me. I think I'm still pissed, but right now, all I can focus on is how grateful I am that we got to you in time and how perfect your little boy is." He turned his pained eyes to me, "Don't keep something like this from me again, Reesie Piecie. He's family, and I want to be a part of his life, as well as yours."

"I'm sorry," I cried. "I wanted to tell you, but I couldn't. You would have told Duke, and I wasn't ready for that." I hiccupped. "I was going to tell him about James. I don't know when, but I wasn't going to keep him a secret forever."

"I know you've been raised to believe the club comes first, and most of the time it does, but with you and me, family will always come first. If I had to choose between being a part of your life or telling Duke, I would have chosen to be a part of your life, both of your lives, and kept your secret. Just remember that, okay?"

That surprised me. The club always came first, or so I thought. "Okay," I sniffed. "I'm really sorry, Carbon. For the record, I missed you, too." My breath hitched with my next words, "Thank you for finding me."

He placed James in my lap and leaned down to kiss my forehead. "I'll always be there for you, little sister, no matter how old you get."

"Knock, knock," a woman said as she wheeled something through the door. She looked vaguely familiar, but I couldn't quite place her. "Hi, Reese. You probably don't remember me, but I'm Leigh, Judge's mom and Duke's aunt." She pushed a pack and play beside my bed. "I brought this for little James to sleep in tonight. Do you want me to get him changed and ready for bed?"

"Oh, yes, that would be wonderful. He'll probably want a bottle first though. He tends to be a little piglet at night. Oh, crap, I don't have any of his stuff here!"

She smiled sweetly, "You do. Judge got his diaper bag when he picked him up from daycare. I ran to the store and bought more of the same kind of diapers, formula, and bottles you had in the bag. As far as clothes, I picked up a few onesies and sleepers for him."

My eyes widened, "Thank you for doing all

that."

"No problem. I remember what it was like to be a young mother around a bunch of bikers. You need all the help you can get. Besides, I just love babies, and your little James is precious."

I smiled proudly, "He is a good baby. He's happy as long as he's fed and gets his cuddle time."

"Treasure it while you can. They grow up too fast," she smiled wistfully, no doubt remembering when her children were small. She picked up James and walked toward the door, "We'll be back and ready for bed shortly."

"Thanks again," I called after her.

Carbon walked toward the door, "I was going to stay with you, but I think, under the circumstances, that Duke should have the opportunity to take care of his boy, should he need something during the night. That okay with you?"

"Yes," I said sheepishly. "Where are you staying?"

"I'll be right next door, and Dash is on the other side of you. Phoenix is on the other side of Dash."

"Thanks, Carbon. Love you, big scary brother," I smiled. I had been calling him that for years.

"Love you, too, Reesie Piecie."

Duke entered the room a few minutes after Carbon left. I couldn't look at him. I was feeling so many different things, and I didn't want any of them to show. I was ashamed of myself for not telling him about our son, but I was still angry with him for the way he treated me a year ago. While I was happy to see him, it also hurt to see him. I was worried he would try to take my son from me, and I was scared because someone tried to kill me. And then there was the person who had been sending me threatening letters since James was born.

I felt the bed shift from his weight when he sat down beside me. He picked up my good hand and brought it to his lips. "Reese, look at me, sugar." I lifted my watery eyes to his. "We've got a lot to talk about and a lot to work out, but I'm not going to walk away from him. Or you."

"Duke, I—" I couldn't find the right words to say, to tell him how much that meant to me, how much I had longed to hear those words from him.

He leaned forward and gingerly wrapped his arms around me, cupping the back of my head with his hand. "Not tonight, sugar. Tonight, just let me hold you and take care of you, both of you. It took years off my life when I saw your car in that tree, with you inside. Then, I damn near had a heart attack when you jumped to Copper as your car fell from the tree." He gently pulled me to him until our foreheads were touching. "I just need to feel you close to me tonight," he whispered.

He leaned back and searched my eyes, for what I don't know, but he must have found it because the next second his lips met mine in a searing kiss. I lifted my good arm to pull him closer to me. Fuck, I missed this man. Duke always felt like home when we were together.

He groaned into my mouth and placed his other hand on my jaw. He tipped my head back so he could deepen the kiss. Things were on their way to getting hot and heavy when we were interrupted by a throat clearing.

Leigh stood in the doorway with our son, sleeping soundly in her arms. "He must have been worn out. He fell asleep during his bottle and didn't even stir when I changed his diaper and put him in new pajamas."

"I think we're all worn out from today," I replied.

"Agreed," Duke said.

I couldn't get up and Duke made no move

to go get our son. Leigh didn't miss a beat. She strolled over to us and leaned down, "You want to give him a goodnight kiss, and I'll put him down for you?"

"Absolutely, thank you for your help tonight." I kissed my boy on his forehead and murmured, "Mommy loves you, little man."

Duke leaned over and kissed his temple, "Daddy loves you, too. Thank you, Aunt Leigh."

"No problem. You two get some rest. I'll be around in the morning if you need me for anything. Goodnight."

When she pulled the door closed, I turned to Duke, "Why didn't you get up and go get our son from her?"

He looked at me incredulously. "Because I didn't want my aunt to see how hard you made my cock, sugar."

"Oh," I muttered. What else could I say?

"Oh," he mimicked.

"Shut it, Duke."

"Go to sleep, Reese."

"Fine."

CHAPTER TEN

Duke

I didn't sleep for shit last night. Every time I closed my eyes, all I could see was Reese's fear filled face trapped in that damn car.

Then, there was the other thing that kept me up. Something I wasn't sure I should mention. Something I pushed to the back of my mind years ago and never thought about again. In my mind, it was like it never even happened.

See, Reese didn't know anyone from Arizona, but I did. I knew a woman with dark, curly hair who lived in Arizona. I wanted to believe it was a coincidence. There was no way she could have found me, and definitely no way she could have linked Reese to me. It was just a coincidence. It had to be.

I walked into the common room, my boy against my chest, and found Carbon sprawled out on one of the couches. "Couldn't sleep either?"

"Nope. The whole thing kept playing over and over in my head. Finally, I said 'fuck it' and gave up on sleep. I would rather be tired than relive my sister's near-death experience over and over again, each time with a different ending."

"Same here, brother," I said as I dropped down beside him and shifted James to my lap.

"How's Reese?" Carbon asked, anxiety evident in his voice.

"She slept through the night and is still sleeping. If she doesn't wake up on her own soon, I'm going to wake her up and give her some more pain meds like Patch said. Don't want her to start hurting so bad we can't get it under control again."

"Good," he shifted, almost as if he was uncomfortable. "Did, um, did you guys talk?"

"Not much. I told her I didn't want to talk about it until later, that I was just glad she was okay."

"Thank you for that. I don't know why she did it, and any other time I would be beyond pissed at her, but right now, I feel the same as you, just glad she's okay," he said honestly.

"She's got a lot to tell us..." I said, trailing off at the end of my sentence.

"Yes, she does. I'm thinking we should start with the threatening letters. It's obvious someone is after her, and I want to know who the fuck they are, and why they thought they could try and kill my little sister," he said, starting to get himself wound up. "I say we get that squared away and then we can find out why she kept your boy a secret. That okay with you?"

I really wanted to know why she kept James from me, but I understood where he was coming from. We needed to make sure Reese was safe first. If she was in danger, so was my son. He could have easily been in the car with her when she was hit. "Yeah, that works. I want to know why probably more than you do, but I get it, safety first."

"She tell you she's moving back to Croftridge?"

I tried to keep the shock, and if I was honest, also the hurt, off my face. "No, she didn't. When did she make that decision?"

He smirked. "She didn't. I did. Surprisingly, she agreed without any argument. Figured we could get what she needs from her house and hire someone to pack the rest of her shit. If Patch okays it, I'd like to head home today. I don't want to be in this town any longer than I have to."

"Works for me. Think we can get Reese out of here without drawing a lot of attention?" I asked. I didn't want whoever was after her to know she was still alive and that she left with us. I had a feeling they'd been keeping close tabs on her.

"Already on that. Batta and Tiny are going to go back to her house to get the things she needs right now. Make it look like they're checking stuff out like they did last night. We'll pull a cage up to the back door and load her and James, then pull out the front gates. Nobody will be able to see them in the back."

"Are they going to stay with you?" I asked. I wanted them with me. They were mine, damn it, even if she didn't know it yet.

He eyed me suspiciously before answering. "I thought it might be a good idea to put them in a room in one of the buildings on Ember's farm. They would be safe there. Most of the brothers are around there as much as they're at the clubhouse. Plus, Ember's there most days, too."

I nodded and kept my thoughts to myself. Mainly, when Ember gave them a room, she would be giving me one right beside them.

***

Hours later, we were on our way back to Croftridge. Reese and James were riding in Patch's SUV with me and Carbon. We loaded our bikes in a trailer we borrowed from Copper along with the items Batta and Tiny had packed from Reese's house. Coal, Edge, and Patch were following us in the other cage with Phoenix and the rest following on their bikes.

It wasn't a long drive to get back home, but I was worried about Reese. She slept through the night, but woke up in a lot of pain. Patch came to the clubhouse when his shift was over at the hospital and gave her a shot to get her pain under control. He reminded her to take her pain medicine as scheduled, not as needed, for the next few days.

James was asleep as soon as we hit the highway. I shot a sideways glance to Carbon. He subtly nodded and began speaking, "Reese, we need to talk."

"I know," she softly replied.

Turning in his seat to face her, he asked, "Why didn't you tell me about the letters?" She gasped, her shock evident. "Oh, you didn't know

I knew about those?"

"No, I didn't. When did you find out?"

"Batta and Tiny found them when they went to your house last night to look for you or clues as to where you might be. How long have you been getting them?"

She cleared her throat and sat up a little straighter, "I got the first one the week after I got home from the hospital with James. After that, I would get two or three a month."

"How were the letters delivered to you?" I asked.

"A few were in my mailbox. They weren't actually mailed to me, someone just stuck it in there. Sometimes they were on the windshield of my car when I left work. The last two were stuck to the front door."

Carbon growled low in his throat, "Damn it, Reese. This psycho knows where you work and has been to your house. Why didn't you fucking say something?!"

"Because I didn't want you to know!" she screamed.

"And why the hell not?" he yelled back.

"Hey," I interrupted, firmly, but not too loudly, "if we can't discuss this without disturbing my son, we will wait until we get back."

Reese turned her gaze to the window and Carbon muttered, "Sorry, brother."

"Sugar, can you tell us why you didn't want Carbon to know?" I asked, keeping my voice soft.

She continued to stare out the window, but she did answer me. "Because I know who they're from, and I didn't want to upset him."

Carbon stiffened in his seat and opened his mouth to speak. I shot him a warning look. I would not hesitate to pull over and put his ass in the other cage if he didn't get his temper under control. My son would not be exposed to a screaming match between his mother and uncle. Not happening.

"Sugar," I said gently, "you know you're going to have to tell us who they're from. Wouldn't it be easier to tell us now, while your brother is contained?"

She snorted at that, then huffed, "Fine. They're from my ex-boyfriend."

My fingers gripped the steering wheel so hard my knuckles turned white. Her ex-boyfriend? When the fuck was this prick her boyfriend?

Rage.

All I could feel was rage. I didn't know if I was more pissed at her or him. She would tell me his name, and then I was going to kill him, slowly. It wasn't her brother she needed to be concerned with: it was fucking me.

"Duke," Carbon barked, breaking my train of thought, "You all right, brother?"

My harsh breathing and flared nostrils were clear indicators that I most definitely was not okay. It came out harsher than I intended, but that couldn't be helped. "Who the fuck is this prick?"

Reese flinched at my harsh tone, then grimaced, cradling her broken arm against her chest. Immediately, I felt like shit. Yes, I was pissed at her, but it wasn't my intention to cause her pain. Carbon's big fist tagged me on the shoulder, "Tone it down, asshole."

Fuck, that hurt. Big bastard. "Right. Sorry, Reese. You okay, sugar?"

"Fine." Oh, hell no, she was not retreating into her one-word answers. I knew she did that shit to hide her emotions and protect herself, but she wasn't doing it this time.

"Reesie Piecie," Carbon murmured, "I need you to tell me who he is."

I heard her swallow and take in a deep breath. She slowly exhaled. "His name is Allen," she paused, seeming to brace herself, "but you know him as Omen."

As soon as the words left her mouth, everything seemed to happen at once. Carbon exploded. Reese jolted and cried out in pain. James woke up, screaming bloody murder. I hit the hazard lights and pulled over. I took my time bringing the cage to a full stop so I didn't jostle Reese around any more and give the others time to stop, particularly Phoenix. I was by no means a small man, but I needed Phoenix, and maybe Patch, to help get Carbon under control.

I jumped out of the cage and bellowed, "Phoenix!"

He was already walking toward the cage, but started running when he heard my shout. When he got closer, I yelled, "Carbon!" and pointed toward the door. We made it to the side of the cage just as the passenger door flew open.

Carbon burst out of the car in a fit of rage, all muscles tensed and flexed. He roared like a wild beast. Phoenix didn't waste one second. He tackled Carbon from the side and took him down to the ground. Phoenix quickly had him on his stomach, but Carbon was fighting like hell. "Get his arms," Phoenix gritted out, using all of his strength to keep Carbon in place.

I grabbed an arm, Dash grabbed the other. Phoenix kept his knee on Carbon's back and used his hands to brace himself on Carbon's thighs. I looked up to see that Coal and Edge had wordlessly joined the fray, each holding a massive calf in their hands.

Patch strolled up like he was taking a leisurely walk on a sunny day. He wiggled the syringe between his fingers and squatted down in front of Carbon's face. "Yes or no?"

Carbon started vigorously shaking his head no. Phoenix barked, "I ain't doing this shit again today. You sure about that, Carbon?"

He didn't speak. He just nodded his in affirmation. Suddenly, Carbon's big body relaxed. It almost looked like he deflated. I assumed Patch gave him the injection anyway, but then I heard her. Reese. Sobbing his name. "Carbon. No, please don't. Don't hurt him. Carbon!"

I dropped his arm and yanked her door open, causing her to almost fall out of the car. She had been plastered against the door, staring down at her brother through the window. I managed to catch her gently and scoot her back into her seat. Grabbing her face with both of my hands, I wiped her tears away with my thumbs. "Shhh. It's okay, sugar. He's okay. Phoenix would never hurt him. None of us would. You know that."

Her lips trembled, her big green eyes were

red from crying. "That's why I didn't want to tell him," she whispered.

Well damn, just who in the hell was this Omen fucker?

CHAPTER ELEVEN

Reese

Phoenix wanted Carbon to ride in the cage with Coal, Edge, and Patch, but I insisted that he get back in with us. When our emotions ran high, we turned to each other. We only had each other after our family was killed. As a result, the bond we formed was unbreakable and, to be perfectly honest, extremely codependent. So, even though he was furious with me, he still needed to be near me just as much as I needed to be near him. For him, it was to make sure I was safe, especially after the bombshell I just dropped on him. For me, I needed to be near him because, unbeknownst to his brothers, I was the only one who could calm him down when his anger took over. Yes, they could restrain him and lock him down until he calmed, but I could stop it in the midst of it happening. I didn't want them drugging him or restraining him when a few words from me could pull him out of the red haze. Had I been able to speak instead of screaming in pain when he first started to rage, Duke wouldn't have even needed to pull over, but all I could focus on was my pain and my baby crying, and the situation quickly got out of hand.

The ride back to Croftridge from that point on was uneventful. We didn't talk about anything related to the letters or the accident. Instead, we discussed what to do with my house in Devil Springs and our grandmother's house in Reedy Fork. That had me wondering where I would live in Croftridge. I hadn't even thought to ask about living arrangements. I assumed I would move in with Carbon like I had before. I was concerned about how I was going to take care of James with one working arm and one working leg, both on the same side, which made balancing a right bitch.

"Has Ember kept you up to speed on what she's been doing with the farm Phoenix inherited?" Duke asked, interrupting my thoughts.

"A little. She said they kept the dairy farm operating as it was, but changed the fake farm into a horse barn and something about growing organic vegetables."

He laughed lightly. "She converted the fake barn into a stable for horses. Blackwings Stables boards horses and gives riding lessons and has recently expanded into breeding and training horses. As far as the organics go, she took a portion of the land and reserved it for growing organic plants and vegetables. She also has a small set-up for hydroponic farming."

"Hydro-what?"

"Hydroponic. It basically means growing plants in nutrient rich water instead of soil. It's pretty cool. I'm sure she'll be happy to show you, or I can."

"Ember did all that?" I asked, surprised.

"She did. She's grown a lot since you left town. Wait, let me rephrase that. She's grown a lot since she came to Blackwings. She's really come out of her shell, and she's done a lot to help the people who suffered at the hands of Octavius, particularly the children. I think that has been her driving force."

Shit. During this whole mess, I hadn't even once thought about having to face Ember. What was I going to say to her? She had no idea that I slept with Duke, got pregnant, and ran off to another town to have his baby, never bothering to tell him, or anyone else. On top of that, I'd been a shitty friend to her since I'd been gone. It had to be that way. If I talked to her and leaned on her, like she did with me, I would've either caved and told her about James, or I would have packed my belongings and moved back to Croftridge. Same thing with Carbon. I had to distance myself. At least until I figured out how to deal with my feelings for Duke.

My feelings for Duke were complicated, to say the least. I wanted Duke. I wanted to be with him and have him be a family with me and James, but I wanted that with the Duke he was before he was stabbed, not the Duke he was after the attack. That Duke was a mean, inconsiderate asshole who didn't want me or our baby and basically told me to move back to Devil Springs. Thinking back on those last few days with him really got my blood boiling. Why in the hell was he here acting like he didn't do a damn thing wrong back then?

Clearly, I couldn't have that discussion with him while my unstable brother was in the car. It would have to wait. I wasn't interested in engaging in a superficial conversation with Duke now that I recalled what an asshat he had been. I closed my eyes and pretended to sleep, hoping he would leave me be.

Blessedly, the remainder of the ride was silent. I opened my eyes when Duke turned off the engine. Looking around, I didn't recognize a single thing. "Where exactly are we?"

"The farm," he replied and shut the door. Carbon must have already gotten out, because he was nowhere in sight.

The farm? I don't think so! Damn that bitch for hitting me with her car. I wanted to storm out of the car and follow him, all the while telling him exactly why he needed to take me and James to Carbon's condo immediately. But I couldn't. Because I had a broken arm and a broken ankle. And a baby I couldn't carry because I couldn't hold him and walk. Damn. Her.

I sat in my seat seething, waiting for what, I don't know, but I refused to move to get out of the car. Fifteen minutes later, Duke opened the back door on the right side while Carbon opened the door on the left. "I'm going to get James out, and Carbon will help you," Duke told me.

"Why are we getting out here?" I asked my brother. Screw Duke. I wasn't talking to him until further notice.

"Duke didn't tell you?"

I rolled my eyes, "Yes, he did. I just wanted to see if your stories matched." I huffed when Carbon remained silent, "No! He didn't tell me."

"You and James are staying here. It's—"

"No!" I yelled. "I want to stay with you!"

"You can't, little sister. I won't be there all the time to help you with James. It's safe here, and there are plenty of people around who can help you while you heal."

"I don't want strangers touching me or my baby!" I shrieked. I was bordering on hysteria.

"Not strangers, Reese. People like Ember, Duke, Dash, and Phoenix; people you know," he explained. He must have sensed my confusion because he continued with his explanation, "Duke works at the stables and has a room out here. Ember and Dash live here, and Phoenix comes by almost every day to visit with Ember or check on the property." He cleared his throat, "They're still finding things hidden around the property."

"I don't want to stay here," I said softly. "It's not my home."

He shook his head. "My home isn't your home either, and you know that. I know what this is about, little sister. No matter where you stay, you're going to have to face Duke, Ember, and even me sooner rather than later. I can't speak for Duke, but Ember will be there for you. She'll be hurt, but she'll still love you as much as she always has. She's missed you. You know I'll always love you, so if it's just Duke you're worried about, I'll go beat his ass right now," he grinned sardonically at me.

"No, don't do that. This just took me by surprise. I was expecting to go to your place or the clubhouse. You know how I don't like things sprung on me at the last minute."

"I'm sorry for that. I thought Duke told you before we left."

"Nope. He definitely did not."

"Well, come on, let's get you inside." With that, he scooped me up and carried me to my new room. The room was larger and significantly nicer than I expected. Ember once described the place as very bland and basic. This room looked like it belonged in a five-star hotel. It was very warm and inviting.

Carbon gently placed me on the bed. "Will you be okay here while I unload your things?"

"I should be. Where's James?" I asked.

"Right here." Duke came through a door I

hadn't noticed carrying my smiling James in his arms. Damn, the sight of Duke holding our baby boy made my ovaries spasm.

"What's through there?" I asked, my voice sounding like it belonged to a wanton harlot.

Damn dry mouth.

Damn sexy Duke.

"The bathroom. It's a Jack and Jill layout. The room on the other side is mine," he told me, smiling.

Oh, fuck no. I was not, for all intents and purposes, sharing a room with Duke. Nope. No way. No how.

He held his hand up, palm out, "Before you say anything, the reason I did that was so James could stay in the room with you, but I would be close enough to hear him and get to him quickly without having to be in the same room as you." Did he just say that? Asshole.

"Ever heard of a baby monitor?" I snarked. He needed to put my baby down and leave.

"I didn't mean it like that, Reese. I figured you wouldn't want me in here with you. I couldn't believe you let me stay with you last night. I knew I wouldn't be that lucky when we got back to Croftridge." He sounded defeated, but I wasn't going to let that bother me.

Ugh, last night. Nope, not going there either. "Yeah, well, you were right about that."

He looked down at the floor and pinched the bridge of his nose. Thankfully, we were interrupted by numerous bikers bringing in box after box after box. I wanted to cry. There was no way I could unpack those boxes. I could barely even walk!

I just sat there staring at the wall until the last box was brought in. Carbon walked to the far side of the room and was back in front of me in mere seconds, placing James in my arms. "You hold the baby. Duke and I will get you unpacked."

I lifted my watery eyes to my brother and sniffed. "Thank you," I whispered.

He kissed the top of my head and got to work. It didn't take them as long as I thought. When they were finished, my room was set up with everything I would need to take care of James, as well as myself.

Duke stretched his arms over his head, making his shirt rise to reveal his chiseled abdomen, which in turn made my mouth water. I wanted to run my tongue over those ridges, again, before I... "I'm going to go get you something to eat. You need to take your pain medicine again. Anything in particular you want?" Duke asked.

Yes, I wanted to lick his abs and do other naughty things to him. "Uh, no, whatever you have is fine."

Carbon chimed in, "How about you see to James, and I'll go get food, yeah?"

When all was said and done, all four of us were full, I had been medicated, and James was fresh and clean and down for the night. Carbon sat at the end of the bed, and Duke was sitting in a chair across the room. Carbon started, "I need you to tell me about Omen."

I sighed. I knew this was coming, but I thought for sure they would wait until the next day at least. "I met Allen the summer before my junior year of high school, about a year before Grandma died. He was a few years older than me and had that bad boy thing going on, so when he asked me out, I said yes. I had no idea who he was. We'd been dating for about 10 months when I found out. When he came to pick me up for a date and I got in the car, I saw something leather laying in the back seat. It was a Mangler's MC cut. We were already moving down the road, and I didn't know what to do. I tried not to react to it and casually asked, 'What's that?' That's when he told me he was the president's son and had just received his patch. He said we were on our way to the clubhouse for the celebration. I yelled for him to pull over and barely made it out of the car before I began vomiting. I'd unknowingly been sleeping with Boar's son for months. When I finally stopped puking, I was a sweaty, stinky, trembling mess. I told him I thought I maybe had food poisoning and asked him to take me home. He did, though it was obvious he wasn't happy about it. After that night, whenever he called, I came up with excuse after excuse as to why I couldn't go out with him. I guess he got tired of hearing my excuses over the phone because he showed up unannounced one afternoon. That's when I told him I didn't want to see him anymore."

I paused and locked eyes with Carbon. "You won't like this next part. Give me your hand." He grimaced and reluctantly placed his hand in my good one. I squeezed it tightly while I spoke the next words. "He beat the shit out of me and left me in a bloody heap on Grandma's front porch. I need you to stay with me, Carbon. Stay. With. Me." I squeezed his hand as hard as I could. I could feel the fury vibrating beneath his skin, but he held it together. I knew he would.

"What happened after that?" Duke asked.

Still holding Carbon's hand, I continued, "After that, I avoided him at all costs. Thankfully, Grandma had gone to visit one of her friends for a few days, so my face was healed enough to be covered with makeup when she got back. I waited a few more days to be sure I could hide if from Carbon. Then, I drove to Croftridge for an impromptu visit. I stayed for two weeks before I went back to Reedy Fork."

Carbon finished the story, "And Grandma died the next day."

"Right," I agreed. I was proud of myself for getting through that story without shedding any tears.

"So, why do you think the letters are from Omen?" Carbon asked.

"Who else could they be from? Look at what they say. It has to be him."

The first one was simple. *Found you.* The cut-out magazine letters were so stereotypical it was almost comical.

The second one was similar. *Can't hide from me.*

I started to get a little freaked out when I received the one that said *You have a Blackwings baby.*

The last one was what sent me into a panic. I

found it under my windshield wipers when I took my lunch break. It said *You and the Blackwings spawn must die.* They didn't know about the last one; it was in the car with me when I got hit.

"You really think it's him after he left you alone for almost two years?" Duke asked.

"Yeah, I do. I guess I wasn't close enough for him to terrorize when I moved to Croftridge, and he started up again when he realized I moved to Devil Springs." I cleared my throat and grabbed Carbon's hand. He instantly stiffened, knowing I was going to say something else he wouldn't like. "Um, you guys didn't see the last one. It was on my car the day of the wreck. It's why I left work early. I was going to Grandma's house to get the pistol she kept beside her bed."

"What did it say?" Carbon asked through gritted teeth.

"It said 'You and the Blackwings spawn must die.'" I squeezed his hand again and begged him with my eyes to stay calm. Shockingly, it wasn't Carbon I needed to worry about.

Duke leaped out of his chair and roared, "He threatened my son and you didn't fucking tell me?!? What the hell is wrong with you, Reese?"

Carbon quickly got to his feet and shoved Duke through the door and into the hallway.

Duke

Thankfully, James stayed asleep.

CHAPTER TWELVE

Duke

I shook Carbon's hands off me and started pacing the hall. How could she not tell me someone was threatening my son? If not me, she should have told Carbon, hell, even Copper. Anyone. She should have fucking told someone.

Carbon started to speak. I whirled around and stomped toward him. "I know she's your sister, and she's been through some shit, but nothing gave her the right to keep my son from me, and she damn sure had no business allowing his life to be threatened without doing anything to stop it! She has two chapters of Blackwings at her back for fuck's sake!"

"I don't disagree, brother, but you need to

hear the story behind her story before you go passing judgment. I know you have feelings for my sister. Whatever those may be, you also have a child with her. When you get to a certain point with Reese, you can't come back from it. Once she has closed the door on you, it's bolted shut, never to be opened again. If you don't want that to happen, listen to me before you act."

I fisted both hands in my hair and roared, "Fuuuuccckkk!"

Footsteps clomping up the stairs had me turning to see a pissed off Phoenix appear. "The fuck is going on up here?"

"We were just having story time, Prez," I spat, my words dripping with venom. Suddenly, I was on my ass.

Phoenix shook his hand out. "Don't give a shit what you got going on right now, boy. Don't you ever take that tone with me."

Fuck me. I was losing my shit. I was showing my ass in front of everyone, screaming and yelling like a damn two-year-old. If that wasn't enough, I disrespected Phoenix, and he had done nothing but be there for me every damn time I'd needed him. I hung my head in shame, "Sorry, Phoenix."

"I know. You just needed someone to knock some sense into you. It's what I'm here for. Now get your ass off the floor and tell me what this is all about," he said, like he hadn't just slammed his sledgehammer fist into my jaw.

He helped me to my feet, and we followed him downstairs to some sort of office. "Have a seat and start talking."

Carbon did most of the talking, telling him everything Reese told us. Then, he filled us in on more. "You both know we don't have beef with the Manglers, but we don't have an alliance with them either. What you don't know is that I have a history with them, or rather my family does, did. Shit, this ain't coming out right."

"Here, this will help." Phoenix slid a shot glass full of amber liquid toward Carbon. Carbon brought it to his lips and tipped it back. Phoenix filled it two more times before Carbon settled back into his chair and started talking. "My mother was Boar's girl when she met my dad. As it was told to me, she wasn't happy with Boar and hadn't been for a long time. She and my dad became friends, and he promised he would protect her if she decided to leave Boar. That assurance was what she needed. She broke things off with Boar, and my dad made sure nothing happened to her. Boar was pissed, but he was too proud to beg her back, so he let her go. My parents didn't get together as a couple until months later, well after she had broken up with Boar, but when Boar found out they were together, he was livid. At the time, his old man was the president and, according to my dad, he told Boar to grow a pair and get over it." Carbon paused and squeezed his eyes shut.

"Keep going, son. I know it's hard, but you're doing good so far," Phoenix encouraged.

Carbon took in a deep breath and gripped the arms of the chair. "Over 20 years later, Boar's old man died, and Boar became the new president. Two weeks later, Mom, Dad, Mason, and Sage were killed. Reese would have been, too, but she was at a slumber party that night. They never caught who did it. Said it was a random home invasion, but I knew, deep down, that it was Boar. I had to identify their bodies and they were, they were just, mangled." He paused and help up one finger, clearly needing a minute to pull himself together before he continued.

"Needless to say, Reese and I had a hard time, a really hard time. I did the only thing I could think of. I was so damn young and didn't know any better. I took her away from Devil Springs, out of school and away from everyone. For six months, her and I traveled around the country on my dad's bike. We went to amusement parks, beaches, lakes, mountains. Hell, we even went on a cruise. Anything I could think of that would be fun and keep our minds off of our dead family. We came back when the next school year was starting. She was going to be behind a grade, but she was okay with that because she was going to be at a new school. After I left her in Reedy Fork with our grandmother, I high-tailed it to Croftridge and refused to talk about any of it."

"That's one hell of a story and full of many things that warrant further discussion, but what does that have to do with her not telling anyone she was in danger?" I asked.

"Don't you get it? I taught her to run away when things were bad and then I reinforced it by allowing her to come visit me without ever questioning the reason behind her unannounced visits. Our family was murdered, we ran off on an epic road trip. Then, I ran off to Croftridge. Omen beat her up, she ran to me. Grandma died, she ran to me. Things happened with you two, she ran to Devil Springs. We didn't give her a chance to tell us her plans, but if we asked her, I guaran-damn-tee she would tell us she was picking up Grandma's gun, picking up her son, and running somewhere else. So, before you judge her too harshly, you need to realize the blame for her actions lies with me." He dropped his head and stared at the floor.

I was at a loss for words. I had no idea Carbon and Reese had been through so much. What he said made perfect sense, but she couldn't run anymore. I wouldn't let her. Not with my child.

Phoenix spoke calmly, but firmly, "You ain't to blame, Carbon. It's a wonder you and Reese turned out as well as you both have given what you've been through. You did the best you could for her at such a young age yourself. Many boys that age wouldn't have done a fourth of what you did for her. You two share a bond that most siblings will never come close to. It wasn't your intention for her to adopt this pattern of running away. It just happened, and you need to let go of that guilt right now so you can help her break this pattern, yeah?"

Carbon's eyes remained on the floor, but he answered, "Yeah, Prez, I hear ya."

"I think that's enough for now. You boys let that girl and her baby rest tonight. Carbon, I'm going to talk about this in Church. Just telling you now so you can get yourself in the right headspace for it."

"Got it."

"All right, both of you get the hell out of my office so I can lock up and go home. I need to sleep for about 15 hours before any more shit gets slung my way," Phoenix said flatly.

With that, I went back to my room. I wanted to check on Reese and James, but I knew I couldn't see her and not say something. Regardless of what Carbon said, I was still irate with her, for so many different reasons. If I was being honest, I was mad at myself, too. I had my own secrets I'd kept from Reese, but the difference was, my secrets weren't hurting anyone. At least I didn't think they were.

CHAPTER THIRTEEN

Reese

I wanted to scream. I was two seconds from pissing all over myself, James was wailing like he had a bee in his britches, and not a damn soul was anywhere to be found. I thought I was staying on this stupid farm because there would always be someone around to help me. What utter bullshit.

I braced my good hand on the bed and used it to help support my weight as I hopped my way around to James. He needed his diaper changed. I knew that cry, just like I knew his hungry cry. Crap. I tried to reach down to rub his head and soothe him, but I couldn't do it without toppling over. I felt like the worst mother in the world. I couldn't do anything for my child except hold him, and even then someone had to hand him to me.

Knock! Knock!

"Please! Come in!" I yelled.

Dash walked in to find me hanging over the side of the crib doing the potty dance. "Everything okay?" he asked skeptically.

"No!" I shouted and hopped as fast as I could to the bathroom. "Get James, I'll be right out!"

I was granted the sweetest relief; my baby stopped crying just as I started to pee. Pure bliss.

I finished my business and hopped back into my room to find Dash holding James and a wide-eyed Ember gaping at me. I cocked my head to the side and raised my good hand to waggle my fingers, "Hi!" I sang to her.

She put her hands on her hips and tried to glare at me, "Reese Walker, you've got some 'splainin' to do."

Ah, shit. I lost it. I fell sideways on the bed and laughed my ass off. Whew, maybe it was time to cut back on the pain meds a bit.

I felt the bed shift when Ember sat down beside me. "Seriously, are you okay, honey?"

"I will be. Can, um, can one of you change James? I can't do it, and I don't know where anybody is," I explained.

"I got him," Dash said. "I'm sure you girls need to catch up." That was the understatement of the year.

"Thanks, Dash." I turned to Ember and put on my best please-don't-hate-me face. "How much do you know?"

"I know about the baby, the wreck, and the injuries. Is there more?"

"Uh, some threatening letters probably sent by my ex-boyfriend who is a member of the MC that likely killed my parents and siblings, but that's it," I said in an almost jovial tone, trying to keep the mood light.

Ember's face fell. She placed her hand on top of mine, "Oh, Reese." She shook her head, silently admonishing me for my actions.

I immediately went on the defensive. "Look, I know I haven't made the choices that other people think they would have made in my situation, but the fact of it is, no one has lived this life but me, and I've done the best I could."

"I'm not judging you. I just wish you would've let me help you, or let anyone help you. No one deserves to go through the things you've been through alone. You were there for me during the most trying time of my life. I would be more than happy to do the same for you. That's what friends are for."

Damn her and her sweetness. She was making my eyes water. I loathed emotional tears. They were always accompanied by feeling the need to vomit.

"Well, I'm here now."

"That you are. Now, introduce me to your son and tell me what you need help with."

Dash walked over and carefully placed James on my lap. "Ember, this is James Mason Jackson. James, this is Ember, the crazy lady you've heard Mommy talk about." Ember gasped. "Just kidding!"

Dash left a few minutes later, giving Ember and me plenty of time to catch up. She told me all about the stables and her organic fruits and vegetables project. She was a huge help, and James seemed to adore her. But the best was when she helped me wash my hair and take a quasi-bath. For that, I would be eternally grateful to her.

"So, how long are you going to be an invalid?"

I scoffed. "Several weeks. My arm isn't that bad. My ankle is another story. I have to go see an orthopedic surgeon in a few days. Patch is supposed to be getting that set up for me. I'll more than likely have to have surgery on it, and then it will be weeks of healing. I'm hoping it won't be too bad once I have use of my arm again."

"You mentioned a crazy ex-boyfriend earlier. Do you think he's responsible for the wreck?"

"I don't know. I would have said yes, but I know it was a woman driving the car and her plates were from Arizona. None of that points to him, but I have no idea who else could have been behind it," I explained.

"Do you know anyone from Arizona other than Duke and Harper?"

"What?" I shrieked. "They're from Arizona? How do you know that?"

"He works at the stables. It was on his new hire paperwork. He used to work at a ranch somewhere out in Arizona before he and Harper moved to Devil Springs. You didn't know?"

I shook my head, mouth hanging open. "No, I did not know that..." I trailed off. Surely, that was just a coincidence, right?

CHAPTER FOURTEEN

Duke

C arbon, Dash, Ember, James, and I sat in the waiting room while Reese had surgery to repair her ankle two days after we brought her back to Croftridge. I don't know who was more nervous, me or Carbon. Both of us were doing a piss poor job of hiding it.

Ember was quietly playing with James while I alternated between pacing the waiting room and sitting in the chair bouncing my knee. If anything happened to her, shit, if anything else happened to her, I wouldn't be able to handle it. This had to go smoothly. I needed her. My boy needed her.

"Family of Reese Walker," Reese's surgeon

called from the door. Carbon and I stood quickly and made our way to him.

"How is she?" I asked at the same time Carbon demanded, "She okay?"

The surgeon smiled. "She's doing just fine. The surgery went better than expected. She had less damage than we originally thought. Still, it is going to be a long recovery for her. We were able to stabilize the joint with a plate and seven screws. I cannot stress this enough; for her to make an almost full recovery, she has to follow the postoperative instructions to the letter. That means no walking on her operative foot for six weeks. None whatsoever. I'm happy to arrange a wheelchair for her, but she previously stated she didn't want one."

"Arrange it. I'll make sure she uses it and stays off her foot," Carbon stated as if it were law.

"Great. Thank you for your help, Mr. Walker. The nurses are getting her settled now, and you should be able to go back and see her soon. Oh, and make sure you bring her son with you when you go back. She was quite adamant about making sure she saw him immediately after she woke up." He smiled and turned to go back into the recovery area.

Getting Reese home from the hospital was a horrid experience I never want to repeat again. She was okay as long as she wasn't being moved, but every bump or sway of the car caused her to cry out in pain. When she cried, James cried, and maybe Ember, too. About halfway home, Reese uttered one word, "Sick."

"Pull over, Carbon, now!" I demanded. He did just that and with little finesse. Reese screamed in pain followed by a choking sound. I quickly pushed her door open and held her steady while she leaned over and threw up nothing but bile. Then, she started sobbing, and she cried the rest of the way home. Holding her to my chest, I tried to soothe her, but nothing I did seemed to help.

When we got her upstairs, I asked Ember to watch James for the rest of the day so I could focus on caring for Reese. Once she had James settled, I climbed into bed with Reese and held her while she slept. I was still angry with her, but I was also glad she was there for me to be angry with.

The first day went pretty much as expected. She woke, took pain medicine, and went back to sleep. The second and third days were much the same with the addition of a little food and drink. By the fourth day, she was ready to get out of bed, but refused to use the wheelchair.

"Reese, you can't put any weight on that foot. You have to use the wheelchair if you want to get out of bed," I insisted.

"The fuck I do," she growled.

"The fuck you do," Carbon stated.

"I can hop on my other foot just like I did before the surgery," she returned.

"Not happening. You could fall and undo all the work they just did and even injure yourself further. How do you think life would be with two broken arms? You want somebody wiping your ass for you?" Carbon gave it right back to her.

She attempted to cross her arms, but with one in a sling, it didn't have the effect she was going for. "Fine," she huffed, "I'll use the chair."

"Ember is on her way up. Carbon and I have to get to Church. I'll be back this afternoon, and then we have Church again tonight," I told her.

She rolled her eyes. "You've met my brother, right? I'm well aware of when you guys have Church." She turned her head away from me and muttered, "Just go."

I should have asked her what was wrong, made her talk to me, but I didn't. I did as she asked and left.

***

We had Church on the same day every week. Since I was the SAA, I had to be there for the meeting with just the officers at lunchtime, and then go back for the meeting with all the brothers later that night.

Phoenix was never one to waste time. As soon as he banged his gavel, we started going over any business issues, revenue, and etc, which didn't take long at all. All of our businesses had been running smoothly the past few months, and we were turning a decent profit, particularly from Ember's new projects. Phoenix addressed Carbon, "I'll do the storytelling for tonight's meeting. Do you want to fill in the officers or you want me to do it?"

"You," Carbon spoke through clenched teeth, "I can't say it all again."

I noticed his knuckles were turning white from the tight grip he had on the arms of his chair. Apparently, Phoenix did, too. "You need to step out until I'm done?"

"Yep." That was all he said before he stood and abruptly left the room.

Phoenix turned to the officers and told them everything going on with Reese, most of which they already knew. Then, he told them the story behind the story of the murder of Carbon's and Reese's family.

"If the Manglers killed Tank and his family, why didn't the club get involved? Why didn't we even know about it?" Badger asked.

"Carbon said there was no evidence that the Manglers did it. He just always believed they were responsible. He could have brought it to me, but he was more focused on taking care of Reese. By the time they got back from their trip, I had moved the club to Croftridge. He had Reese set up with their grandmother and she was doing okay, so he pushed his suspicions to the back of his mind and focused on moving forward. Honestly, I think he completely blocked it out, but it all resurfaced when he found out Reese had been dating Omen," Phoenix explained.

"That's why he flipped out like he did on the way back from Devil Springs," I added.

"What's the plan?" Badger asked.

Phoenix rubbed his chin with his thumb and forefinger. "We've got a couple of things to deal with. First and foremost is Reese's safety and health, as well as that of her son." I cleared my throat. "Which is also Duke's son, but I believe all of you already knew that." He shot me a sideways glance. "Then, we've got the issue of someone intentionally pushing Reese's car off the side of a mountain and the threatening messages she's been receiving. Last but not least, regardless of who's behind those things, Omen still beat the hell out of her two years ago. I don't give a fuck if it was two days, two years, or 10 years ago, he will answer for that, feel me?"

Everyone at the table readily agreed. Not a one of us were okay with a man hitting a woman, not like that anyway. Sparring in the ring or slapping an ass in the bedroom was a different story.

"For now, Reese is safe at the farm. That place has top-notch security and there's at least one brother on the premises at all times. Still, I'm going to send Coal to stay out there and keep an eye on things. He's familiar with the place since he grew up there. Containing Reese shouldn't be a problem while her mobility is severely limited. I'm going to get in touch with the police officers in Devil Springs and see if they have any new information for us regarding Reese's wreck. Also, I'm going to ask Copper if his boys can keep an ear to the ground and an eye out for anything to do with the Manglers. Byte, see what you can dig up on the Manglers, particularly Boar and Omen. Oh, and see what you can get on yellow

Nissan Xterras with Arizona plates driven by a woman. There can't be that many. Anything else?"

I shifted in my chair. I should say something. I needed to tell them. It could be affecting my son's safety. Fuck! "I've got something."

All eyes shot to me. I looked around and thanked my lucky stars that Carbon hadn't returned to the room.

"Spit it out," Phoenix ordered.

"Uh, I'm not sure if you guys were aware, but before Harper and I moved to Devil Springs, we lived in Arizona, and I know a crazy bitch with dark, curly hair who lives there. It could be a coincidence, but I think it's worth checking out," I uttered. My mouth was so dry I could hardly swallow.

"Go on," Phoenix urged.

I cleared my throat and wiped the beads of sweat from my forehead. Shit, there was no going back now. "Her name is Shannon Jackson. She's my wife."

The door burst open. "You motherfucker!" was bellowed behind me before my ass was handed to me by none other than Carbon.

CHAPTER FIFTEEN

Reese

I hated that fucking wheelchair. Hated. It. After Carbon unceremoniously placed me in it and left, I made the decision to stay in my room for the next few weeks. The staples had been removed from my head, as well as the stitches in my leg, so I had no need to leave my room until my next appointment. I felt like an idiot rolling around in the motorized contraption. It sounded very much like a golf cart every time I pressed the little joystick to make it move. People could hear me coming for miles.

Ember walked into my room and interrupted my internal tirade. "Guess what?" she squealed, way too chipper for me to handle.

"Fair warning, you should tone it down a bit if you're going to be spending the day with me," I sniped.

"Oh good, you're pissy. I have just the thing to turn your frown upside down."

I cocked my head to the side. "Did you just say pissy?"

She nodded enthusiastically. "Yes, I did. If you can pull the stick out of your ass, I might say something else, too."

"Like ass?" I giggled.

"No, like fuck!" she shouted.

I threw my head back and laughed so hard I almost peed in my chair. My stupid fucking chair.

"Good, you're laughing. Let's go." After issuing her command, she picked up James and walked out of the room.

"Where are we going?" I shouted after her. "In case you didn't know, this fancy piece of equipment can't go down stairs."

She yelled from down the hall, "If you hurry it up, you can get on the elevator with us."

Elevator? Hell, yeah. I had been going stir crazy in that room. Despite my previous vow to stay in my room, I really needed a change of scenery. I was not one to sit around cooped up and enjoy it. I jammed my little joystick forward as far as it would go hoping to catch up with them.

I made it to the elevator to find Ember grinning at me like a loon. "Oh, hello, Reese. Would you like to join us? I was going to take young James here to the stables to see the horses, and then give him a tour of the organics farm."

"Why, yes, I would. Please make way for a very bad driver to enter your domain." I wasn't kidding. I was not doing a bang-up job driving the chair, or maybe I was doing a bang-up job. I hit the wall four times before I made it to the elevator.

"Whoa! Stop, stop!!" Ember screamed, causing James to giggle. The little turd. "Doesn't that thing have brakes?" I had Ember pinned against the back wall of the elevator, while she held James high in the air out of harm's way.

I shrugged. "I don't know. It's not like anyone gave me driving lessons. My big bastard of a brother plopped me in it and left. Hell, I don't even know how to make it go in reverse."

Ember laughed. "This is going to be hilarious. I need to get my phone. You wouldn't mind if I recorded this, right? I bet I can get you into one of those Epic Fail videos."

I shot her my most menacing glare. "Don't you dare or so help me when I get out of this chair..." I trailed off and let the threat hang in the air.

"You know I wouldn't do that to you. I was just trying to make you laugh. I know this really, really sucks for you." She paused for a moment. "I'll make a deal with you. I'll try to make the next few weeks better for you if you'll try to not make them so bad, yeah?"

I rolled my eyes. "I'll try, but I'm not promising anything."

She showed us around the stables and the organics farm. She had accomplished a lot in the last year. I was beyond impressed. It really was good to see Ember doing so well after everything she had been through. Anyone who met her would be able to see how happy she was. I was truly happy for her, too, but it also made me wonder if I would ever have that kind of happiness in my life.

"Oh, there's something else I want to show you. You're going to love it!" Ember said excitedly.

I followed her to some building not far from the stables. Luckily, there were no stairs, so I could roll right in the front door. She walked to a room on the far side of the building, did something with a bookcase, and the freaking wall opened up. She turned back to me, "It's a secret tunnel!"

I sat, mouth agape, staring at the opening to the tunnel. "What? Why is it there?"

"I don't know. Octavius was crazy is the only reason I can come up with. We've found things like this all over the property. We're actually still finding things."

"Where does it go?" I asked.

"This one doesn't go anywhere anymore. It used to lead to Octavius's house, but my dad had that demolished not long after he inherited the property. Do you want to go in and check in out?"

"Is it safe?" Yes, it was cool, but it also seemed dangerous, and I wasn't about to put James in harm's way.

"It is. Dad and Dash both forbade me from entering any of the secret passageways until they were deemed safe by an inspector. Not all of them were safe, so those have been clearly marked with caution tape. This one is fine though, I promise."

"Well, okay then, let's go."

I rolled into the secret passageway behind Ember. It was creepy to say the least. The pathway was equipped with motion detector lights, but they weren't very bright, making it difficult to see more than a few feet in either direction. The walls were made of some sort of metal which made everything sound funny.

We'd been in the tunnel for 10 minutes or so when James started fussing for his afternoon bottle. Ember placed him in my lap while she got the bottle out of the diaper bag hanging on the back of my chair. She reached to get him but I stopped her. "It's okay, I can feed him."

"Are you sure? I don't mind."

"Thanks for offering, but this is one of the things I can do for him."

She patted me on the shoulder before leisurely walking along the passageway, studying the walls and the floor while James drank his bottle. I stayed put. There was no way I could maneuver my chair and feed him at the same time.

My boy had just finished his bottle when Ember disappeared right before my eyes. I gasped. She screamed. "Ember! Ember!" I shouted. I couldn't see her, but I could hear her, or something, making noise. I couldn't tell where it was coming from.

Fuck.

Fuck.

Fuckity fuck.

I didn't know if I should stay and try to look

for her or go get help. When James cried out, I knew what I had to do. As much as I wanted to look for her, I had to get my baby out of there. It clearly wasn't safe. It's not like I could do much to help her anyway. The best thing to do was to go get help.

I wasn't sure if she could hear me, but I yelled it anyway, "I'm going to get help, Ember! Just hang on!"

I threw James's empty bottle to the ground and resituated him as best I could in my lap. Then, I slammed the joystick forward and prayed I could get back to the office without crashing. The wheelchair didn't seem to be going as fast as it was that morning. I needed it to go faster, but it didn't. Instead, moments later, the damn thing died, right there in the tunnel.

That was when I completely lost it. I didn't have my cell phone with me because I didn't think I would need it. I couldn't walk by myself, let alone while carrying James. Ember needed help, and I was as helpless as I was useless. Great big sobs wracked my body, tears splashing onto James's fuzzy head. James began crying the moment I did. He didn't like it when his mommy was upset.

"What are we going to do?" I sobbed. Despite

my best efforts, I couldn't seem to calm down. I felt trapped, just like I had been in my car. Just like then, all I could do was wait for someone to find me. Only this time, I had James with me.

I don't know how long it took, but, eventually, I managed to calm down and James drifted off to sleep in my arms. I hadn't heard any noises since I started to go for help and I didn't know if that was because I was too far away to hear anything, or if Ember wasn't able to make the noises anymore. Fear consumed me as I sat in the dark tunnel. Then, that fear slowly morphed into anger.

Every second I sat there I grew angrier and angrier. Years' and years' worth of pent-up anger boiled to the surface. Why were my parents and siblings taken from me? Why was my Grandma taken from me? Why did Omen have to hurt me? Why did Duke have to treat me like shit? Why was someone threatening me? Why did someone try to kill me? Why was more shit happening to me? What did I ever do to deserve any of this?

CHAPTER SIXTEEN

Duke

Fuck. Carbon beat my ass good. And I let him. I didn't even try to fight back. I deserved it, and I knew it. It took all of the officers to pull him off of me. Phoenix was beyond pissed when they got us separated. He ordered us to stay out of each other's way until further notice. I wasn't sure how that was going to work, seeing as how his little sister was my child's mother, and she needed both of us to help her while she healed.

My head was throbbing, and my whole body ached. Whatever Patch gave me for the pain wasn't doing a damn thing to help. He wanted me to go to the hospital, but there was no way that was happening. I knew my nose was broken and at least one of my ribs was cracked. They couldn't do shit for either one of those injuries.

Banging on the door caused my head to throb harder. "Duke! Duke! Get the fuck out here, now!" Dash yelled through the door. More banging. "Carbon! Out to the common room. Now!" A feeling of dread settled deep in my gut. If he was yelling for both of us like that, it could only mean one thing. Something had happened to Reese.

Despite the pain, I was on my feet and out the door in a matter of seconds. I didn't stop in the common room, even when Phoenix yelled my name. I learned from the last time Reese was in trouble to not waste a single second. I ran out the front door and jumped on my bike, flying out of the lot with a spray of dust and gravel.

I wasn't surprised in the least when Carbon's bike pulled up right beside mine. We rode side by side hauling ass to the farm. I had no idea what was wrong, but I needed to get to my woman and my boy.

We skidded to a halt in front of the building that held our rooms. Coal came running outside when he heard us pull up. "The girls are missing! Neither one of them are answering their cell phones, and no one has seen them in hours." He was panting, his eyes full of panic. "I've got anyone I could find looking for them!"

"Where was the last place they were seen?" I demanded.

"Sarah that works with the hydroponic plants said they came by there a few hours ago. She didn't know where they were headed, but I haven't found anyone who has seen them since," he told us.

"Keep gathering everyone you can. We'll go building by building, room by room until we find them," Carbon stated just as Dash, Phoenix, and the rest of the officers rolled up. Carbon filled them in on the plan and we quickly divided up the buildings, sending two people into each to start searching room by room.

Phoenix paired off with Carbon, I assumed to keep him under control, while Dash and I headed to the building assigned to us. I had not realized just how big the farm was until I had to comb through it inch by inch searching for someone.

I entered another room to find absolutely no one. Where in the hell could they be? I knew they wouldn't have gone off the property. I'm not sure Reese could have even if she wanted to.

The next room I entered was L-shaped. At

first, it just looked like a regular office, then I rounded the corner. Shock and disbelief coursed through me. There, between the bookcases, was a fucking tunnel. They wouldn't be so stupid, would they? Of course they would.

"Dash! Get in here!" I bellowed.

He ran through the doorway. "Did you find them?"

I pointed to the opening. "Think they're in there?"

His face reddened, and his fists clenched. "Probably," he gritted out as he headed into the tunnel.

It was dark and creepy as fuck. We walked deeper and deeper for several minutes, lights turning on as we passed. Then, I saw them. Reese and James. On the ground. I started running. "Reese! Are you okay? What happened?"

Her head popped up, and she looked right past me. "Dash! Ember! That way! She disappeared. Look for the bottle!" She was pointing and screaming, not making any sense.

"Slow down. What are you trying to say?" he asked.

"Ember disappeared when we stopped to feed James. She was standing there one second, and then she just vanished. I threw down his bottle so I could hold him and drive the chair to get help. Go find the bottle!" she screeched.

He took off at a sprint through the darkness. She turned her gaze to me, "Go help him."

"No. I need to make sure you and James are okay," I insisted.

"We've been here for hours, Duke! A few more minutes won't change anything. Go fucking help him!" she screamed.

I didn't want to leave them, but I also wanted to help Dash. Thankfully, the decision was made for me. "I got her!" Dash yelled from down the tunnel. "She's okay!"

"All right, let's get you two out of here," I said gently, reaching to pick up my son.

Reese pinned me with her fiery green eyes. "I want my brother." What the hell? Was she mad at me?

"Are you angry with me about something?" I carefully asked.

"Get my fucking brother!" she shrieked.

James jolted in my arms. Not wanting the situation to escalate, I relented and called Carbon. "We found them, and she's demanding to see you. Won't let anyone else get near her." I told him where we were and that was it. He never said a word, just disconnected the call. I knew he would be here soon though. If anything, he would always come when Reese called.

Not even two minutes later, Carbon and Phoenix came barreling down the pathway. By this time, Ember and Dash had joined us. Reese refused to say anything to anyone other than when she asked for Carbon. He dropped to his knees beside her. "Are you okay, Reesie Piecie?"

"No, no I am not. Can you carry me back to my room? The wheelchair battery died. You can leave it here for all I care, but I would like to get out of this hellhole."

He hoisted her up, careful not to jostle her leg or her arm and started walking toward the exit. I heard him ask if she needed Patch, and I breathed a sigh of relief when I heard her say no. Otherwise, neither one of them said a word to the rest of us.

"What the fuck was that?" I uttered to no one in particular.

Ember shook her head. "I don't know. I've never seen her like that. I've seen a lot of her moods, but nothing like that. I don't know what happened between me falling through the wall and now." She looked up at me and gasped. "What happened to your face?"

"Another time," Dash murmured. She nodded

and didn't say anything else about it.

"I'm going to head back to my room. You guys coming?" I asked.

"No, not yet. Ember fell into a hidden room, one we had yet to find. There are some things in there that we need to look through. You go ahead, but call if you need us," Phoenix said. "Dash and I will bring the wheelchair over to Reese when we're done here."

With that, I left.

***

The following few weeks were hell, to say the least. Reese would hardly speak to me. I tried several times to talk to her, but each time she told me to leave and threatened to call her brother if I didn't. I wasn't scared of Carbon. Yeah, he was bigger than me and would likely whoop my ass, again, but I wasn't afraid of him. I did, however, respect him, so when she asked me to leave, I did. Even though she didn't want to have anything to do with me, she did let me see my son whenever I wanted.

I felt like I was stuck, like my life was on hold, and there was absolutely nothing I could do about it. We hadn't been able to track down the person or the car that ran Reese off the road. We had nothing on the Manglers, no suspicious activity, no rumors circulating about them. Boar and Omen kept to their clubhouse most of the time. As if that wasn't enough, my fucking wife had dropped off the face of the planet. Byte couldn't find that bitch anywhere. That in itself was disturbing. Byte could find anything. So, until we got a lead on one of our issues or Reese decided to acknowledge my existence, everything was on hold, at least for me.

I was sitting at the bar at the clubhouse trying to drink my problems away when Phoenix dropped onto the stool beside me. "You doin' all right, brother?"

"Just fine," I uttered.

"Don't sound like it. Don't look like it either," he observed.

"No disrespect, but I don't want to discuss it." I really didn't. I didn't want everyone at the bar to hear my business. The brothers gossiped worse than the Old Ladies and club whores.

Phoenix nodded. "Ah, I see." He stood and gestured toward the hall. "Follow me to my office."

He didn't ask, so I figured I didn't have much of a choice. I got my ass up and shuffled toward his office.

I unceremoniously flopped into a chair, my glass of whiskey almost empty. Phoenix reached into a desk drawer and pulled out a bottle of the high dollar stuff he kept hidden from the rest of us. He gestured toward my glass. I swallowed what was left and placed it on his desk. He filled it half way and slid it back to me. "Sip on that while you listen."

I picked up my glass and took a sip. Phoenix started talking. "I know what you're going through right now, probably more than you think. You feel like you're at a standstill, right?" I nodded. "That's how it is for me with Annabelle, not knowing what happened to her, if she's dead or alive. There's no telling how much shit we've yet to discover hidden away out there on that land. Every time we find something new, I think it's going to be the time that I find something that will bring her back to me. Then, it turns out to be nothing to do with her, and I'm right back where I started. I can't move on until I've gotten her back or let her go, and I can't do that until I know what happened to her."

He paused and brought his own glass to his lips. "Ember would understand, too. I know she and Reese are tight, but you could trust her to keep things to herself if you asked her to."

He paused for a moment and studied me. "You know why her and Dash haven't gotten married yet?" I shook my head. I had no idea why they hadn't had the wedding yet. "Because she's waiting to find out what happened to Annabelle, and that just tears me up inside. It's one thing for my life to be on hold, but her life just started, literally, and now it's on hold because I can't find her mother. But this ain't about me nor her right now, it's about you. I just wanted you to know there are people around this place that are in that same boat with you."

I swallowed, my throat feeling clogged with emotions. "Thanks, Prez." I looked down at my glass and twirled it with my fingers. "Reese won't talk to me," I uttered before I could stop myself.

Phoenix's eyebrows rose. "Why not?"

I shook my head, keeping my eyes on the floor. "I'm not sure. She's been angry, really angry, since we found the girls in the secret passageway. I don't know what happened in there, but I've been on her shit list ever since that night."

"Did you talk to Carbon about it?" Phoenix asked.

"No, we haven't seen much of each other since

you told us to stay away from each other."

"Shit, Duke. I didn't mean it like that. I just meant for a week or so, until you both calmed down some. Go talk to him. He knows her better than anybody."

"I'll think about it."

"Don't think about it. Do it. Better yet, go talk to Reese. If you want her, go get her and tell her how you feel. At least she's right here in front of you, alive and almost well."

Shit, he was right. There I was moping about Reese, when all I had to do was go talk to her. He didn't know if the love of his life and mother of his child was dead or alive. "Thanks, Phoenix, appreciate it."

I was going to make her talk to me, but not tonight. I already had too much to drink to go anywhere and this was a conversation we needed to have completely sober. With nothing else to do, I went back to the bar and kept drinking.

CHAPTER SEVENTEEN

Reese

"You don't know how good this feels," I squealed as Ember drove me back from the doctor's office. He removed the cast from my arm and gave me a splint to wear if needed. He also put me in a walking boot and gave me the green light to start using my ankle again, slowly at first, but still, no more wheelchair.

I had refused to even look at it after being trapped in the passageway, but I finally realized that I had to use it if I wanted to do things like use the bathroom by myself. I still didn't use it much, and I never left my building. I wasn't going to end up in another situation where I was trapped because the damn battery died. In short, I didn't trust the stupid chair. I couldn't wait to send it back.

We got out of the car and I picked up my son. Cradling him in my arms, I walked to the front door with a huge smile on my face. It was a simple action, one many mothers do every single day, but for me, it was a moment I would cherish forever. I propped him on my hip and tottered toward the stairs.

"Let's take the elevator. You know, just to be on the safe side," Ember hesitantly called out.

I frowned, but turned and tottered to the elevator. I wanted my full independence back, but she was right, I shouldn't push my luck. I damn sure didn't want to end up back in a wheelchair.

I fed James and put him down for his afternoon nap. "Do you mind listening out for him? I'm going to take a shower, and I'm going to enjoy every second of it."

She grinned. "Go on, you deserve it."

I did enjoy every second of that shower. I stayed in there until I ran out of hot water. I deep conditioned my hair and shaved everything that needed shaving. I was afraid the amount of hair I removed was going to clog the drain.

Things south of the border had gotten a little out of hand, but I couldn't shave and balance with one good arm and one good leg. As much as I loved Ember, I was not going to ask her to shave my hoo-ha for me.

Dressed in only a thin tank top and shorty shorts, hair wrapped in a towel, I entered my room to find a wide-eyed Ember and a fuming Harper staring at me. Well, fuck me sideways, what was Duke's sister doing here? And why the hell did she look pissed off at me?

"Harper, what an unexpected surprise. What are you doing here?" I asked, feigning nonchalance.

"Really, Reese?" she shrieked. "You and my brother have a baby and no one bothers to tell me?"

"Shhh!" I hissed. "You'll wake him up." I glanced back at James to make sure he was still sleeping. "I'm sorry, I didn't know Duke hadn't told you."

She scoffed. "I find that hard to believe. Didn't you think it was odd that I hadn't come to see my nephew?"

Seriously, she needed to have this conversation with her brother, not me. "Honestly, Harper, no I didn't think it was odd because you didn't even cross my mind. I was a little busy healing from my near-death experience a few weeks ago. You know, when my car was pushed off the side of a mountain by some deranged lunatic."

She gasped and covered her mouth with her hand. "What?" she asked shakily.

I rolled my eyes. Her scaredy cat routine wasn't going to work on me. "You should really talk to your brother about this."

Her lower lip started to tremble. Oh, give me a break. "I will," she quietly said, "but can I see him first? I promise I won't wake him; I just want to see him."

I gestured to the crib. "By all means..."

I knew I was being unreasonably catty toward Harper, but she caught me off guard, and her accusatory tone immediately put me on the defensive. Plus, I was still pissed off at her brother. He was hardly around, so I was directing my hostility at her.

"He looks just like Duke," she whispered.

"Yeah," I agreed, "he does."

"I can't believe he kept this from me," she said, sounding hurt.

Crap, she was making me feel bad, and I really shouldn't care what she thought. I wanted to let her think Duke kept it from her, but for some unknown reason, I just couldn't do that. "He didn't know about James until six weeks ago.

I can't say why he hadn't told you in that time, that's something you will have to ask him."

"He didn't know you were pregnant?" she gasped.

"No, he didn't. I was going to tell him, but things happened and he was— You know, I really don't want to discuss that part with you. It is what it is. I didn't tell him, moved away, had the baby, had a wreck, and he found out when the daycare called him. That's the short version; Duke can fill you in on the details."

"Do you know where he is? I thought he was working today, but I went by the horse barn, and no one was around. He didn't answer his door either."

"I don't have a clue where he is. Did you call him?" I asked.

"No, I didn't want him to know I was coming," she explained.

"Okay. Thanks, Dad," Ember said, cell phone in her hand. She looked over to us. "He's at the clubhouse. Do you want me to drive you over there?"

"Yes, thank you. Reese, are you coming, too?" Harper asked, begging me with her eyes.

"Nope. I don't want to take James to the clubhouse this late in the day, especially since it's the weekend. There's too much smoke and other debauchery for him to be around."

"I bet Coal's mom would be happy to watch him. She loves little James." Thank you, Ember.

I flopped down on the bed and started combing out my hair. "Fine. Call her and see."

Thirty minutes later, we dropped James off with Mrs. Martin and were on our way to the clubhouse. I didn't want to see Duke, but knew I inevitably would. That meant I had to dress carefully. I wanted to look good, but not look like I tried to look good. I wore my cutoff jean shorts and a black Blackwings MC tank top that was probably a size too small, but did wonderful things for my boobs. Since the outfit was so casual, I did my eye makeup a little heavier than usual. Leaving my hair down, I styled it in subtle beachy waves. For the first time since the accident, I felt good about myself.

That feeling lasted until we walked into the common room of the clubhouse. I knew they would be having a party; they always did on Friday nights, but I thought they would just be getting started since it was only a few minutes after 8:00 pm. Apparently, they had gotten started a little earlier than usual. Several of the brothers already had club whores in their laps or crawling all over them, most of which were barely clothed. One of those brothers was none other than Duke.

Fuck.

This.

Shit.

"There's your brother," I snapped at Harper and gestured toward the fuck nugget with the whore on his lap. "I'm out." I turned with a wobble and did my best to storm off down the hall.

I was not going to cry. We weren't together. He could do whatever or whoever he wanted. I just didn't want to see it. I needed a drink, but there was no way in hell I was going back in the common room. Not just because of Duke. I also noticed a whore pawing at my brother and trying to climb in his lap, which meant it wasn't safe for me to go hang out in his room. Damn it. I never should have agreed to come with them.

I pushed through the back door, hoping no one was fucking in the pool, and breathed a sigh of relief when I didn't see anyone else around. Closing my eyes, I tilted my head to the sky. Why was my life so complicated?

"What are you doing out here?" a deep voice asked from behind me, close behind me.

I screamed and whirled around, nearly falling over thanks to my booted foot. "Shaker! You asshole, you scared the hell out of me!"

He grinned. "Yeah, that's what I was trying to do."

"Bastard."

"Brat."

"Go away."

"But I brought you something. You don't want it?" he asked, taunting me.

I didn't have the patience for his crap. "What is it?"

He handed a bottle to me. "Tequila."

"Hell, yes! You got limes and salt?" I asked, my night suddenly looking up.

"Of course." He reached inside his cut and pulled out two limes, a salt shaker, and a shot glass.

"I think I'm in love with you."

"I know. My thoughtfulness and my handsome face make me irresistible. Oh, and let's not forget my rockin' body." He flexed his biceps and smiled widely.

I couldn't help but giggle. He could be standoffish at first, but once you got to know him, he was hilarious.

We sat down at one of the patio tables. He

pulled out his pocket knife and cut up one of the limes while I opened the bottle and filled the shot glass.

"You get the first one. I think you need it more than me anyway," Shaker said.

"What makes you say that?" I asked before picking up the glass and taking the first shot. I hissed. "I always hate the first one."

"Wuss." I refilled the glass for him. He tipped it back with no fanfare. "I was in there when you came in. Saw what you saw. Grabbed the tequila and followed you out here."

I grabbed the shot glass and muttered, "I don't want to talk about it," right before downing my second shot.

"You sure about that?"

"Yes. Pour me another." He did, and then again, and again, and again.

"I think that's enough for now, Reese."

"Why?" I slurred and swayed. "I'm only seeing two of you. I thought the cutoff was at three." I clapped my hands together and cackled into the night. I was damn funny when I was drunk, at least I thought so anyway.

Shaker shook his head. "Your brother is going to kill me."

"My brother is probably balls deep in a club

whore's ass right now, yanking her hair and making her scream for mercy. If he's thinking about you, there's a problem." I arched a brow and tipped my chin down slightly. "Know what I'm saying?"

His face contorted in disgust. "Oh, shut the fuck up, Reese. I don't want to know anything about what Carbon does with his dick, and it damn sure doesn't have anything to do with me."

"Methinks he doth protest too much."

"Methinks your ass is about to get tossed into the pool."

I clumsily lifted my foot and waggled it at him. "You can't. Nana-nana-boo-boo."

"Brat."

"You called?"

He rolled his eyes and huffed. "Note to self. No more tequila for Reese. Ever."

I stuck my bottom lip out and pouted. "Oh, come on, Shaker, I'm just teasing you. I've had a rough time of it lately and I need to blow off some steam."

"Yeah, yeah. Use me and abuse me." I almost didn't hear the last part because he said it so quietly. "Just like the rest of them."

"What was that?"

"Nothing." He sat up straighter in his chair.

"So, why did you come to the clubhouse tonight?"

"Pour me another shot and I'll tell you."

"If you puke on me, I'm tossing you into the pool, booted foot or not."

"Deal." I put my hand out to shake his. He laughed but shook my hand. "Harper showed up at the farm looking for Duke. She found me and Ember instead. She was furious and demanded to know why no one told her about James. I told her to talk to her brother about that, so here we are."

He sat quietly for a few minutes. He leaned back in his chair and cocked his head to one side. "Can I ask you something?"

"You just did."

"Such a smartass." He chuckled. "Why didn't you tell Duke about the baby?" I opened my mouth, but he put up a hand to stop me. "I'm not passing judgment; I'm honestly just curious. I know you, and I know you wouldn't do something like that without a good reason."

"You're right. I did have a good reason..." I trailed off. "I don't mind telling you, but it needs to stay between me and you right now. This isn't a club thing, and I don't want every member knowing my business."

"Got it. Does your reason affect the club in

any way or is it strictly personal?"

"Strictly personal."

"Then you have my word that it stays between us."

I cleared my throat. I had never uttered this story to anyone. Most of the time I tried to pretend like it didn't even happen. "When Duke was in the hospital last year, I was at the hospital all the time. We weren't officially together, but we had something going on, and I had feelings for him. I thought he had feelings for me, too. When he woke up from his coma, he was like a completely different person. He was so mean and hateful to me. Some of the things he said to me I could never repeat. Some cut me deeply and, I guess, rang true in a way." I paused, trying to gather my strength to continue.

Shaker scooted his chair closer to mine and wrapped his arm around my shoulder. "You don't have to tell me any more."

"I want to. I think I need to. I've never told anyone about this, and I think it might be good for me to get it out."

"That's up to you, sweetheart."

I took a deep breath and continued. "He told me I was a mistake. That he wished he'd never touched me. He said I was a child with a woman's body, and he was disgusted with himself for having ever laid a finger on me. He told me he knew I had feelings for him, and I needed to get that shit out of my head. We would never be together. He said he wasn't interested in playing house with a little girl, especially one that had daddy issues. If that wasn't enough, he went on to say it was my fault he was in the hospital in the first place because I was the one who brought Ember to the club. He said I was too stupid to see the danger she was bringing with her and not only did I almost get him killed, I could have destroyed the whole club. He ended by saying I should do the club a favor and disappear." I pushed myself off his shoulder and turned to face him. "So, that's what I did. I disappeared and 'played house' by myself."

Shaker's jaw was clenched, lips pressed into a thin line, fists balled, and face red. Crappity crap. He spoke through gritted teeth, "Your brother know about this?" I shook my head. "Phoenix?" I shook my head again. "That motherfucker," he growled.

"Shaker, you gave me your word."

"I told you it would stay between us, and it will, but I never said I wouldn't beat his ass and not tell him why."

"Please, don't do that," I cried. "I told you because I needed to talk to someone and get it out, not so you would do something about it. Beating his ass isn't going to change anything. It's not going to undo the hurt he caused when he said those things to me."

"I just can't believe that motherfucker. First, we find out he has a wife no one knew about and now this shit!" Shaker barked.

Any buzz I had was instantly gone. I froze, hearing nothing but my own heartbeat as my mind tried to process his words.

Lub-dub.

Wife.

Lub-dub.

Duke.

Lub-dub.

James.

Lub-dub.

Stepmother.

Lub-dub.

No! I needed my happy place. I needed to not feel. I needed my brother. I needed to breathe. I felt Shaker shaking me, and I was vaguely aware of him speaking, but I couldn't understand what he was saying to me. Finally, I got one word out. "Carbon," I croaked.

"Come on, sweetheart, I'll take you to him." Shaker lifted me into his arms and ran into the clubhouse.

"No! Not in there!" I wanted to scream, but I couldn't get the words out. I tensed up in Shaker's arms and frantically shook my head back and forth.

"I'm taking you to my room. Then, I'll go get your brother. Try to slow your breathing, Reesie Piecie," Shaker rambled.

He placed me on his bed and I closed my eyes, focusing on my breathing and the heartbeat pulsating through my ears.

Wife.

Wife.

Wife.

"Reese!" I heard Carbon's frantic voice, but I refused to open my eyes. I needed to find the place in my head where I didn't feel, where nothing could hurt me, where I was safe. "What the fuck did you do to her?"

"Nothing, man. We were outside talking, and she just shut down. I was taking her into the common room to find you, and she freaked out, so I brought her in here."

They continued talking. I heard more voices join in. Ember, Dash, and maybe Phoenix. I tuned them out. If I kept my eyes closed and blocked them out, I would be okay. I wanted everyone except Carbon to leave. Why wasn't he making them leave? He knew what I needed when I got like this. Then, I heard him.

HIM.

Duke.

I sat straight up, opened my eyes, and said one word, "Wife."

CHAPTER EIGHTEEN

Duke

She said one word. Just that one word destroyed any hope I had of talking to her and working things out between us.

"Wife."

I felt like a knife had been plunged directly into my heart. I took a staggering step back, still staring at her beautiful face. A face filled with so much pain. Pain that I put there. "Please, Reese, let me explain."

"You need to go. Right the fuck now," Carbon ordered, stepping in front of me.

Fuck this shit. He wasn't going to stand in between me and Reese anymore. Brother or not, this was between me and her. "No, you're the one who needs to leave." His chest puffed out, but I kept going, "This has nothing to do with you. We have shit we need to talk about, and you aren't going to stand between us anymore. Don't you get it, Carbon? She's not fragile and delicate. She's fucking hiding behind you! That shit needs to stop. Now!"

He was trying to control his temper, I'll give him that, but he barely had it under control. "I'm her brother," he gritted out. "She can hide behind me anytime she wants to, for whatever reason, from anyone, including you. Now, get the fuck out."

"I'm not leaving. Not until I talk to her."

Surprisingly, Shaker pushed Carbon out of the way and stepped in front of me, his face filled with rage. "Didn't you say everything you needed to say to her last year, *brother*?" He said brother like it left a nasty taste in his mouth, like he was disgusted by me, and, from the look on his face, I guessed he was.

I looked to the ground and shook my head. "Fuck," I muttered, more to myself than anyone.

"What the fuck are you talking about?" Carbon demanded.

Shaker looked directly at Carbon. "Promised

her I would keep it to myself, man. If she wants to tell you, she can, but I'm not going to betray her trust. Sorry, brother."

Carbon looked at Shaker with respect in his eyes. "Got it." He turned his angry eyes to me. "You want to fill in the gaps, assface, or should I start breaking bones?"

"ENOUGH!" Phoenix roared. "Everybody out of this room. Right the fuck now!"

We all stood there unmoving, stunned by Phoenix's outburst. "If this room isn't cleared in 10 damn seconds, I'm shooting whoever's still in here!" He reached around behind him, I assumed to pull his gun from his pants, which meant he was serious. I didn't wait around to find out. Everyone poured into the hallway and Phoenix slammed the door shut, leaving only him and Reese inside.

Movement to my right caught my eye. I turned my head to see my sister cowered in the corner, shaking like a leaf. Fuck. I was screwing things up left and right. I started to go to her, to try to comfort her, but to my utter disbelief, Carbon strolled over to her and pulled her into his arms. What in the everloving fuck? Before I could question it further, Phoenix opened the door.

"Duke, you can come in." I looked back and

forth between him and my sister being held by Carbon. Reluctantly, I stepped into the room with Reese and Phoenix.

I dropped into a chair and Phoenix began, "Now before either one of you says a word, I want you both to keep your mouths shut and listen. This is a fucking motorcycle club, not a damn daytime soap opera. I can't have brothers beatin' the hell out of brothers, girls crying and passing out, friends and family members swinging on club whores. We've got way more important things to deal with than that type of bullshit. But most importantly, you two have a child together. You're going to have to deal with each other in some form or fashion until one of the three of you dies. That may sound harsh, but it's the truth, so in the best interest of James, I'm going to help you two talk some shit out, or I'm kicking both of your asses out of my clubhouse, got me?"

Holy shit. In all the years I'd known Phoenix, I'd never heard him say anything like that to a brother. I sat up straighter in my chair. "Got it, Prez."

If looks could kill, Phoenix would have died 10 times over from the glare emanating from Reese. She crossed her arms and huffed, "Whatever."

"Wrong answer. You want to try again, or you want to get the fuck out?" Phoenix barked.

Her eyes widened in surprise. "Got it."

"Good. Now, everyone knows you both have feelings for one another. That was made perfectly clear by how you both reacted when the other's life was on the line. Either one of you want to attempt to deny that right now? A simple yes or no will do."

I knew Reese wouldn't want to answer first. She hated showing her emotions. It was time for me to nut up. "No, Prez."

Phoenix gave me a chin lift and turned his eyes to Reese. She didn't say anything, but she shook her head.

"So, what's the problem?"

"She was going to have an abortion!" I said at the same time Reese said, "He has a wife!"

"Anything else?"

"She kept my son from me!"

"He called me a little girl with daddy issues and said he didn't want to play house with me!"

"Ah, now we're getting to the root of the problem, or roots I suppose. Yes or no answers only. Reese, were you going to have an abortion?"

She honestly looked shocked at the question. "No. I would never..." she trailed off when Phoenix narrowed his eyes.

"Duke, do you have a wife?"

Fuck me. I had to answer without being able to give an explanation. Through gritted teeth, I forced the word through my lips, "Yes."

"Reese, did you keep his son from him?"

"Yes."

"Duke, did you say you didn't want to play house with a little girl with daddy issues?"

"Yes."

"So, I'm just taking a stab at this, but I'm going to venture to say that Duke said he didn't want to play house because he thought you were having an abortion. Reese kept your son from you because you said you didn't want to play house with her. How am I doing so far?" Phoenix smirked at the both of us.

"Sounds about right for my part," I muttered.

"Mine, too," Reese added.

"All right, forgive me for being blunt, but how long has it been since you two fucked?"

I stood. "That's none of your damn business, Phoenix, and you know it."

He chuckled. "That long, huh? Okay, Duke, you need to explain why you thought she was going to have an abortion and give her a chance to tell you her side. Then, you need to tell her about your very estranged wife. Last, but not least, you two need to fuck each other and be happy." He clapped his hands together once and strolled toward the door, "My work here is done."

I looked at Reese, so much pain and anger evident in her eyes. "Will you let me explain about my wife, please? I promise it's not what you think."

"Isn't that what all cheaters say?" she sniped.

I felt the corner of my mouth lift in a half-smile. "I suppose you're right about that, but this time it's the truth. Will you just hear me out?"

"Seems like I have to." She waved her hand toward the door. "Orders from the president and all."

"This isn't something I like to talk about. Ever. And I'm not going to go into a lot of detail about it. When Harper was a kid, she was kidnapped. Our family never had a lot of money. We were lower middle class I guess. Anyway, our mother had just passed away after years of battling cancer. The cost of her treatments and the funeral expenses left my dad with next to nothing. The police were getting nowhere with Harper's case. A month had gone by, and I was getting desperate. I knew money talked, so I did what I had to do to get it. Shannon had been after me for years, and her family was disgustingly rich. So, I married her and used her family's money to find Harper. By that point, our father had drunk himself to death grieving over the loss of his wife and then his daughter. When I finally found Harper, we got the hell out of Arizona and never looked back. I didn't tell anyone we were leaving or where we were going, including Shannon. I haven't seen or heard from her since we left Arizona."

Reese remained silent for several excruciating minutes, digesting everything I said. "Why are you still married to her?"

I sighed. "This is going to make me sound like a complete idiot, but it's the truth. I sort of forgot that I had married her."

Reese stiffened. "You forgot? How could you forget you had a wife?"

"Because I didn't give a shit about her. I only married her so I could use her family's money to find Harper. We were only married for a few weeks before I found Harper and split. Then, I was focused on being able to provide for Harper and making sure she was okay mentally."

"Did you sleep with her?" she calmly asked, a little too calmly for my liking.

I studied her face, looking for a hint as to what

she was getting at. "Does it really matter if I did or didn't?"

"Yes," she answered flatly.

"Not that it's really any of your business, but yes, I did. And not that I should have to explain myself, but I had to fuck her so she wouldn't know what I was up to. She had to think I really wanted to marry her."

"So, you married the girl, used her for sex and money, and then left her swinging in the wind when you got what you wanted. Does that sum it up?"

"It wasn't my finest moment, Reese, and I'm definitely not proud of my actions, but I would do it again in a heartbeat if I had to. I love my sister, and I had to find her. Marrying Shannon was the fastest way to get Harper back. And you're assuming Shannon is this delicate little flower that I crushed. She's not. She's a cold, calculating, crazy bitch. You of all people should realize that."

"Why would I realize that?" she asked, puzzled.

"Because she's the one who ran you off the road!" I blurted.

"What?" she shrieked. "How do you know that?"

"I don't know it for sure, but she is from

Arizona, she has dark, curly hair, and, like I said, she's a crazy bitch."

"Why would she come after me? I thought you hadn't seen or talked to her in years."

"I haven't. My best guess is she found out you and I have a child together, and that pissed her off. How she found out is anyone's guess."

"So, what are you going to do about her now?"

I sighed and ran my hands over my face. "I figured I would let the police handle it, and, of course, I will happily divorce her, but I have to find her first."

"You're telling me no one can locate this psycho bitch?"

"That's what I'm telling you. She has the means to make it hard to find her, but we'll get her eventually. That I can promise you."

"We'll see. So, what's next on our list of topics we've been ordered to discuss?" she asked, a hint of sarcasm in her tone.

"The abortion," I stated bluntly. "I heard you on the phone saying 'He doesn't want it and neither do I' and 'I don't care about the money, I just want to get rid of it quickly.' Then, you had a doctor's appointment the next day. Care to explain that?"

"How did you even know I was pregnant?" she

asked.

"I wasn't awake yet, but I could hear people talking. I heard Harper ask you if you were pregnant because you kept getting sick and you were having dizzy spells. You quickly denied the possibility, but I knew by the sound of your voice that you were lying to her."

"I see. Well, about what you heard me say on the phone; I was talking about selling my grandmother's house. I was explaining that I didn't want it and neither did Carbon. The real estate agent was telling me all sorts of things we could do to get more money out of it. I explained that I didn't care about the money, I just wanted to get it sold quickly. I did know that I was pregnant, and I was freaking out about money. As for the doctor's appointment, I went to confirm the pregnancy and get some medication for morning sickness."

I looked down at my hands in my lap. I had made a huge mistake. Fucking huge. I said things to her that I knew would destroy her and send her running far away from me, all because I jumped to conclusions instead of acting like an adult and talking to her about it. "Reese, I need to apologize for what I said to you in the hospital. I was already so angry about being stabbed, and when I thought you aborted my baby, I was fucking furious. I wanted to drive you away, so I said the things I knew would do that. I didn't mean any of it. Swear on my life, I didn't mean a word I said. You have to know that."

I looked up when I heard her sniffle. Tears were streaming from her vivid green eyes.

I moved to sit next to her on the bed, caressing her cheek with my hand. "I'm sorry, sugar. I know how much those words hurt you, but I promise you, I didn't mean them. I don't expect you to forgive me, but please know I didn't mean a damn word I said."

Her breath hitched when she started to speak. "That's why I left, and that's why I didn't tell you about the baby." She began sobbing. "I thought you didn't want us. I was going to tell you about him eventually, but I wanted to prove to you that I wasn't a little girl, that I could do it on my own if I had to."

I pulled her into my arms and held her while she cried. "I'm so sorry, sugar. So sorry," I murmured to her, gently rocking her back and forth.

When her sobs quieted down, I shifted so I could pull back and see her face. Even with her eyes red and puffy from crying, she was still the most beautiful woman in the world. I met her eyes and bared my soul. "I do want you. I've always wanted you. And now, I want both of you. You good with that, sugar?"

She whispered the word I desperately wanted to hear, "Yes."

My lips met hers with raw, animalistic need. I grabbed the back of her neck with one hand, sliding my fingers into her silky hair. My other hand went straight to her perfect ass. She braced herself with her hands on my shoulders, squeezing just enough for me to feel her fingernails through my shirt. I groaned at the sensation. It had been over a year since we were together, and I had been longing for her ever since.

"Duke," she whimpered against my lips.

"What is it, baby? What do you need?" I asked, never taking my mouth away from her. I trailed kisses along her jaw and down her neck, waiting to hear her answer.

"You, Duke. I need you," she moaned.

I leaned forward and carefully positioned her on her back. She was a sight to behold laid out before me. Her tank top was doing nothing to conceal her hard nipples, and her short as hell shorts were barely keeping her perfect pussy covered. My mouth watered at the feast before me. "Get that shirt off, sugar," I demanded while I pulled mine off and tossed it to the floor.

She immediately tensed and crossed her arms over her stomach. "Duke," she said softly, "I'm not the same."

My cock was hard and throbbing, begging to be inside her. It was all I could focus on. That, and getting my mouth on her tits. "Of course you are. Shirt off. Now." I reached for the hem of her shirt. If she didn't want to do it, I would.

She slapped my hand away. "No, Duke. I want it to stay on." She turned her head to the side so she wasn't looking at me, but she held onto the hem of her shirt like it was a lifeline.

I took a deep breath and forced myself to calm down. Obviously, something was at play here. "Reese, baby, talk to me. What's going on?" I planted my hands on the bed on either side of her face and hovered above her.

"I'm not the same as I was. I had a baby. I don't look like I used to or like those girls running around out there," she mumbled.

"Sugar, I don't look the same either, but you know I don't give a damn about any of that. I've always thought you were beautiful, but that's not why I'm with you. Knowing your body changed to give life to my son, fuck, that makes me want you even more."

She shyly smiled. "You're with me?"

I growled, "Damn right I am. Now get those gorgeous tits out. I want to suck on them while I slide those hot ass shorts and your sexy panties down."

She hesitantly pulled her tank top over her head and popped open her front clasp bra. She was right. She wasn't the same. Her tits were bigger, and I couldn't have been happier about that. I dove right in, latching onto one nipple with my mouth and clasping the other between my fingers. "Oh, baby, I love your tits," I uttered.

I slowly slid a hand down her stomach until I reached the button on her shorts. Quickly, I popped it open, lowered her zipper, and divested her of her shorts and panties, being mindful of the boot on her foot. I kept my mouth on her nipple, alternating between sucking and biting, while I slid two fingers into her tight, wet pussy. I pumped them in and out twice when she started gasping and digging her fingernails into my back.

"Damn, baby, I wanted this to be slow and sweet, but it's been too long." I undid my pants and pulled my cock out, rubbing the head along her slick slit.

"Please, Duke," she whined.

"Please what, baby?" I loved it when she begged. She did it every time I fucked her, and I couldn't get enough of it.

"Please fuck me, Duke. Please fuck me hard and make me come all over your cock. Please. Please. I need you to fuck me."

Music to my ears. I stood and pulled a condom from my wallet before I shoved my jeans and boxers to the floor. Once I was covered, I climbed between her splayed thighs and slid my cock into her all the way to the hilt on the first thrust. "Fuck," I hissed. "You feel so fucking good, baby. You're going to have to come fast, I'm not going to last long. Fuck. I need to move, yeah?"

"Please. Fuck. Me. Now. Duke."

I dropped my mouth to hers while I pulled almost all the way out and slammed right back in. I could already feel the tingle in my spine. Slowing my pace, I tried to think of anything that would help delay the inevitable.

I had things under control until I looked down to see Reese rolling her nipples between her fingers. Fuck me. I was going to come, and there was going to be no stopping it. "You like playing with your tits, dirty girl?"

"Yes," she groaned.

I pulled back so I could rub her clit while I continued to pound into her. "You gonna come for me?" I lightly smacked her clit once, twice, and that was all it took. She screamed as she came, her pussy clamping down on my dick so hard I swear I saw stars. I pumped into her harder while she rode out her climax, and then I was shooting my own release into the condom.

I collapsed on top of her, my dick still just as hard as it was before I fucked her. I took a minute to catch my breath, and then I started moving my hips, gliding in and out of her, slowly this time. I framed her face with my hands and softly kissed her lips. "I've missed you so much, sugar."

She ran her hands over my sweat soaked hair, and then wrapped her arms around my neck, pulling me down to her. "I missed you, too, Duke. More than you know."

"I'm not letting you get away again. I'll make things right, and we'll raise our boy together. I promise."

"Okay, Duke." I could hear the smile in her voice. I turned my head toward her, kissing along her jaw while I held her tightly to me.

I continued moving, softly thrusting into her. It occurred to me at that moment that I was making love to a woman for the first time in my life. I pulled back. I wanted to see her eyes when I said, "Reese, baby, I l—"

She cut me off, "Don't say it now. Please." The desperation in her tone had me agreeing to her plea without questioning it.

"Okay, sugar." I captured her lips again and didn't let them go until we both came down from our second orgasms.

For a second, I was worried things would be awkward or uncomfortable between us, especially after my almost declaration of love, but Reese eased my worries when she said, "You know Shaker is going to kick your ass for fucking me on his bed."

We both burst out laughing. "Yeah, you're probably right about that. Let's get dressed and get out of here."

I held on to the condom while I slid my thankfully deflated cock out of her. When I came back from the bathroom, Reese had a strange look on her face. "Reese? You okay?"

Her expression changed into her well-known mask of indifference. "Yes, I'm fine."

"Don't bullshit me. If something's bothering you, tell me. Don't shut me out."

She pulled her shirt on over her head and

moved the sheets to cover her lower half before she said, "I didn't like that you had a condom in your wallet. I know I have no right to say anything about it. You've been free to do whatever you wanted, but—"

"That's been in my wallet since the day after your prom. I haven't been with anyone since I was with you the first time."

"You can't be serious. You had a club whore on your lap not even two hours ago."

I snorted. "You walked in at the right, or wrong, moment. She'd just plopped her ass down when you came through the door. You ran out of there so fast you didn't see me push her onto the floor. I promise, baby, no one since you."

I wanted to know, but I didn't want to ask. Thankfully, she voluntarily shared the information I craved. "I haven't been with anyone since you either."

"It feels like there's something else you're not saying." She seemed nervous and that was completely out of character for Reese.

"At the beginning of my pregnancy, I had to have all the tests done, and everything came back fine. So, I'm clean, and I'm on birth control now, and I was thinking if you were clean, too, maybe we could not use those."

"I'm clean, sugar. I had to have a complete physical when Ember hired me to work at the stable." I paused for a moment, then asked a question that probably wasn't my place to ask, "Why are you on birth control now?"

"Um, I had a difficult delivery when I had James. The doctor said that I shouldn't get pregnant for at least one year, preferably longer, and recommended birth control."

My chest hurt. She had a difficult delivery, and I wasn't there for her. "Was anyone there with you? When you had him?"

"A friend from work was with me. My water broke at work, and she drove me to the hospital. When she found out I didn't have anyone coming to the hospital, she stayed with me."

"I would have been there if I had known."

"I know. Let's not talk about it anymore. What's done is done, and we can't change it."

"Okay, sugar. You ready to go?"

"Yep, I'm going to toss Shaker's sheets in the wash, and then I need to find Ember to tell her I'm leaving with you. I'll come find you when I'm finished."

CHAPTER NINETEEN

Reese

I closed the lid on the washing machine and turned around to find Ember, Harper, and Phoenix surrounding me, all with matching looks of dread on their faces. Fuck! "What happened?" I croaked.

I'd seen that look before, more than once. That was the look people had when they were about to tell you something that was going to destroy your life. "Tell me!! Duke? Carbon? Who is it?"

Nothing could have ever prepared me to hear the next words that left Phoenix's mouth. "Neither. It's James."

Everything stopped. The sounds in the

clubhouse dissipated. My vision blurred. My chest tightened. My heart exploded with pain. A scream of sheer terror erupted from me as I collapsed to the floor. "Nooooooo!!!! Not my baby!!!" I gasped for air and started to fold in on myself. Massive arms scooped me up, and then we were moving.

"Just hang on, Reesie. The boys have already left. They're going to get him back. You just hang in there. He's going to need you when they find him," Phoenix said into my ear while he carried me down the hall.

"He's alive?" I whispered.

"Far as I know," he answered.

He gently placed me on Carbon's bed. Normally, Carbon's room was my safe haven, but this time I wanted to be in Duke's room. "Can we go to Duke's room?"

"Anything you want, Reesie." He scooped me up again and off we went to Duke's room.

I picked up his pillow and squeezed it tightly to my chest. "What happened?"

"I don't know the details, but the short of it is he was taken from the Martins' house. Coal stopped by his parents' house and found his mother on the floor trying to crawl to the phone. He called as soon as she told him what happened.

That woman wouldn't even let him help her off the floor until he called here."

"Is she okay? Does she know who took him?" I asked.

"She's at the hospital, pretty banged up, but she should be okay. She's beside herself about James though. She didn't know who took him, but she said it was a woman and gave us a description." He paused and looked down. I already knew what he was going to say.

"It matches the description of the woman who hit me, right?" I guessed.

"Yeah, darlin', it does."

I pushed to my feet. "Fuck this. I'm not sitting around this clubhouse crying while some crazy bitch has my baby. Ember, give me your keys."

"Wait just a second," Phoenix said, now on his feet, too. "I can't let you leave, for a number of reasons, but before you flip your shit, listen to me. I really hoped you would never have to know about this, but that Blackwings pacifier clip that Duke brought home for James, it has a GPS locator in it. We put one on his infant carrier, too. Duke insisted on it after you guys were stuck in the tunnel for hours. We know where he is, and the boys have gone to get him."

I couldn't believe what I was hearing. "You

put a GPS locator in my baby's pacifier clip and on his car seat?"

"Yeah, we did and I ain't going to apologize for it," Phoenix firmly stated.

"I don't want you to. Thank you so much!" I launched myself at the big man and hugged him tightly. "Thank you, thank you, thank you." Any other time, I would have likely been pissed, but at that moment, I was just grateful they knew where my son was.

Phoenix actually blushed a little. "Gotta say, Reesie, definitely not the reaction I was expecting out of you, but I'll take it."

"Can you find out if they've gotten to him yet or where they are? Please," I begged.

"Of course. Come with me." I followed him down the hall and into Byte's room. "You got an update, brother?"

"You're not going to believe th— Oh, hey, Reese, didn't see you there," Byte stumbled over his words when he saw me.

"You can speak freely in front of her right now. I'm not going to believe what?"

"It looks like she's headed to the Manglers clubhouse with the baby," Byte told us.

I gasped. No, no, no. They would not get their hands on another member of my family.

"Fuck!" Phoenix roared. In the next second, he had his phone to his ear. "Copper, got an emergency, and I need your help."

CHAPTER TWENTY

Duke

There I was hauling ass on my bike, a-fucking-gain, with Carbon riding right beside me. He might be the club's enforcer, but when we caught this bitch, she was mine. Woman or not, she was going to pay and pay dearly for taking my son.

My phone rang, scaring the shit out of me. I still wasn't used to my new helmet. It connected to my phone via Bluetooth so I could answer calls while on the road. Phoenix insisted we all upgrade to them a few months ago. I wasn't crazy about it at first, but now I was damn glad we'd made the change.

"Answer."

Phoenix's voice filled my ears. "Looks like they're heading toward the Manglers clubhouse. Could be a coincidence, but I'm not taking that chance. Copper and his crew are going to spread out and block all possible routes leading to the clubhouse. There's not many, so it shouldn't be hard to get her if that's where she's going."

"Are you fucking serious?" I growled.

"Yep. Keep it together, man. You can fly off the handle after you get your boy back. I haven't told Carbon, and I'm not going to until you guys are back here. He'll flip, and that can't happen right now."

"Got it. How far ahead of us are they?"

"You're closing the distance, but I think Copper and his boys will get to them first. Just keep pace with Carbon. Byte has a line open with him telling him where to go."

I was afraid to ask, but I had to know. "How's Reese? Did you tell her?"

"I did. She's right here with me and Byte. She's doing okay, staying strong for her boy, isn't that right, sweetheart?"

Her voice was like a balm to my aching soul when she called out, "Bring him back to me, Duke." Then, she morphed into the Reese I knew so well. "And bring that bitch, too. She's got an ass-kicking waiting on her."

"You hear that, brother?" Phoenix chuckled into the phone.

"Got it, Prez." He disconnected the call. Surprisingly, my focus was solely on the road in front of me. Occasionally, Carbon would accelerate and lead the way when we needed to make a turn, but otherwise, we rode side by side with the cavalry behind us.

We sped past the scene of Reese's accident. Chills went up my spine as we passed. I still had nightmares about that night. Every single time, James was in the car with her, and I had to watch as they plummeted to their death. I forced those thoughts from my mind. I needed to focus. We were getting close, and I couldn't let the memories of that night distract me.

Finally, a group of motorcycles surrounding a car came into view. We came to a stop, and I don't know how my bike didn't hit the ground. I jumped off and ran as fast as I could toward the group of men. They parted as I approached. There, in the middle of the fray, was my cousin holding my baby boy. And he was just fine.

I plucked James from Judge's arms and cradled him against my chest, kissing the top of his head. "Thank God you're okay, little man.

Your mommy and I have been so worried about you." I'm not ashamed to say a tear or two fell from my eyes. We could have easily lost him.

I took a moment to rein in my emotions and turned to face my Devil Springs brothers. "I can't thank you enough for getting my boy out of harm's way."

Copper clapped me on the shoulder. "It's what we're here for. Family is family and we always take care of our own." Then, he shrugged, "And we were having a boring night anyway."

"Shit, I need to call Reese." I shifted James to my hip and reached for my phone.

"I already did, as soon as we had him out and looked him over," Judge told me.

Carbon had been standing silently beside me the entire time, which could only mean one thing. Carbon was in full enforcer mode. His tone held a promise of pain. "Where's the bitch?"

"She's over there," Copper pointed, "but I don't think it's who you were expecting."

We walked over to the woman bound and gagged on the ground. Carbon used the toe of his boot to roughly roll her over. I couldn't believe what I was seeing. "Melissa? What the fuck are you doing here?"

She bared her teeth and snarled at me like a

rabid animal. "Oh, you can't answer that, can you? Well, we'll just leave that gag in place until we get you to a more desirable location."

"You know this cunt?" Carbon barked.

I sighed. "She's Shannon's sister."

CHAPTER TWENTY-ONE

Reese

For the second time that night, my knees hit the floor. This time due to sweet relief. They got my baby back, and he was okay.

"I'm going to need you to stop doing that. You're making me look bad when I don't catch you," Phoenix grumbled.

"Sorry, Phoenix," I sassed. I knew he was trying to help me keep my emotions from getting the best of me.

He helped me to my feet and led me to the common room. I was surprised to see the room relatively empty. He handed me a shot of whiskey and explained, "Everybody went after James except me, Byte, Ranger, and a couple of prospects. Coal's at the hospital with his mom."

"She's really okay?" I asked. Mrs. Martin was one of the sweetest women I knew. I hated that she had gotten hurt because of me.

"She's banged up, but she'll be fine. I know what you're thinking and don't go there. It ain't your fault."

I shook my head. "Duke was right. I do only bring trouble to the club," I mumbled. I hadn't really intended to say that out loud and I hoped Phoenix didn't hear me, but I had no such luck.

"The fuck you just say?" Phoenix barked. "He said that to you?"

"A long time ago. He's since apologized for it, and said he didn't mean it, but I can't help thinking it's true. Every time I show up here, chaos ensues," I explained.

"I think you failed to realize that you didn't show up here either time. You were ordered to come to the clubhouse when everything happened with Ember, and you were brought back here after your accident. We're your family, Reese. We'll always be here to help you no matter what."

"He's right you know," Ember said from behind me. "You are family, and I, for one, am so glad you're back."

Harper slowly crept toward the three of us. "I'm sorry for yelling at you about the baby when I first got here. I just want Duke to be happy, and it seems you make him happy." She smiled softly and pulled me into a hug.

"Okay, enough of the sappy shit. You all know how I hate that," I griped.

"It'll be a while before they get back here with James. You girls want something to eat?" Phoenix asked.

"I do," I quickly answered. "I'm going to need my strength to beat that bitch's ass when she gets here."

Phoenix chuckled. "So, steak and potatoes?"

***

The doors to the common room flew open to reveal Duke standing there like a dark knight holding our sleeping son. Damn the boot on my foot. I wanted to run to him, but it was a fast hobble at best. When I got to him, he handed James to me, and I lost it. I placed kisses on the top of his head and all over his face. I cried, dropping tears and snot all over his little head. Duke silently stepped forward and wrapped us in his arms.

We stayed in his arms for several minutes. When I finally got a hold of myself, I pulled back a little and met Duke's eyes, "Thank you."

He smiled softly. "You don't have to thank me, sugar. I'm his dad, it's my job to protect him. Go get your things so we can get him home."

I shook my head. "Not until I have a chat with the bitch that took him."

"You're not going to budge on that, are you?" he asked, already knowing the answer.

"Hell, no."

He sighed. "Fine. Ember, can you watch James for us?" I stiffened when he asked her. It's not that I didn't trust Ember, but my son had just been kidnapped while in someone else's care. I didn't exactly want to leave him with another person just yet. "You're not taking James down there. He'll be just fine while you handle your business."

I handed James off to Ember and followed Duke down the stairs that led to the cells where they had once kept Ember. Duke stopped suddenly causing me to slam into his back. "Wait right here. I'm fucking serious, Reese. Don't move from that step." The tone of his voice was something I hadn't heard from him before.

"Okay." What the hell was he doing? He went

down the rest of the stairs and walked out of my line of sight. I couldn't make out what he was saying, but I could hear him talking to some of the other brothers. Moments later he was back, motioning for me to come down the stairs.

"What was that about?" I asked.

"Club business," he grunted.

Whatever. I really didn't care. I just wanted to knock this cunt's front teeth out and be on my merry way.

He led me into a cell. A woman was tied to a chair with a gag in her mouth. She was younger than I thought she would be. Significantly younger. "This is your wife? How old was she when you married her, like 10?" I shrieked.

"No, she's not my wife. This is my wife's sister," he explained.

"Why the fuck would she take my son?" I asked, utterly confused.

"Don't know yet. Didn't want to waste any time getting James back to you, so we haven't questioned her yet."

I hobbled over to her and removed the gag. "Why did you take my child?" The stupid, stupid bitch spat in my face. "Oh, that was the wrong thing to do." I raised my hand and slapped her across the face, then brought the back of my hand across her other cheek on the downswing.

I quickly moved behind her and grabbed her ponytail, using it to yank her head back so she couldn't spit on me. "Do you know where you are?"

She grunted in response. So, she wanted to make this difficult. I looked over to Duke. He was leaning against the wall, arms crossed over his chest, watching me curiously. "Can you get my brother for me, please?" I asked sweetly.

Carbon entered the cell. "You rang, little sister?"

"Hello, big scary brother. Could you get me some ice water, please?" I stared at him and innocently batted my eyelashes a few times, hoping he understood my request.

Carbon grinned menacingly and nodded. He returned with two five gallon buckets of ice water and a thin, damp cloth. I yanked her head back by her hair and placed the cloth over her mouth and nose. At my nod, Carbon lifted one of the buckets and slowly poured the ice cold water over her face. She thrashed, sputtered, gagged, and coughed, but she couldn't get away. The water just kept coming.

Carbon paused and I asked, "You ready to talk?"

She clamped her lips shut, and we started again. This bitch would talk, one way or another. By the time we got started with the second bucket, we had attracted an audience. Only the officers were allowed down in the cells, but every single one of them was there. To my surprise, Copper and a few of his crew were also watching.

Finally, halfway through the second bucket, the bitch uttered through blue lips, "I'll talk! I'll tell you everything! Just please stop!"

"You have two minutes to get it all out or we start again," I said in a tone that even unnerved me.

"My sister is missing. She came out this way looking for Duke. She's getting married, and she needed him to sign the divorce papers. She was afraid they would get lost in the mail, or that he wouldn't sign them, so she came in person. About two weeks ago, I got a letter in the mail that said if I wanted my sister back I needed to come to Croftridge. I was given instructions once I got here. They wanted me to take the baby and trade him for my sister. I was just trying to get my sister back," she cried.

I wasn't buying the bullshit she was selling. "Why didn't you call the police?"

"The letter said not to tell anyone. It said if I

did, my sister would die," she explained.

"Do you have any proof that someone actually has your sister?"

She nodded frantically, "Yes, I talked to her on the phone."

I arched a brow and looked at my brother. He was right there with me. I turned back to the psycho. "She was allowed to talk on the phone?"

"Just the one time. It wasn't for very long, maybe not even a minute," she rambled.

"Where were you supposed to trade my son for your sister?" I asked in a calm voice. I was on to this bitch. I was casually propped against a table, well out of spitting distance. My brother was circling the room slowly, a predator ready to pounce.

"I, I, I don't know. They gave me an address, but I have no idea where it was. I was just following the GPS directions," she stuttered.

I turned and caught Copper's gaze. He was beaming at me proudly. I mouthed the word phone to him. His smile widened, and he stepped forward, placing her cell phone in my hand. I knew one of them had it. They would have searched her car and taken anything that might be useful.

I kept my back to her and turned on her

phone. The idiot didn't even have it password protected. Byte could have bypassed it anyway, but that wasn't the point. I opened up her text messages and only read one message before rage consumed me.

Her phone fell to the floor. I whirled around and let my fists fly with everything I had. I couldn't hit her very hard with my left arm, but I did what I could. My right hand, however, was fair game. The impact of my third punch tipped her chair backward, sending her crashing to the floor. I was mid-leap when Carbon snatched me out of the air. I struggled against him, clawing and hissing like a feral cat, but my strength was no match for my monster-sized brother. "What the fuck, Reese?"

"She was taking my son to the Manglers. Her sister is Boar's Old Lady!" I screamed.

"Carbon, get her out of here. Duke, lock that bitch down. Everybody upstairs. Church now!" Phoenix bellowed.

CHAPTER TWENTY-TWO

Duke

What the fuck? Shannon was Boar's Old Lady. How did that even happen? Don't get me wrong, I never gave a shit about Shannon, but I didn't for one second believe this was all a big coincidence.

"I think we know why we haven't been able to track down Duke's wife. On the bright side, now we know where she is. This would also explain why we haven't seen or heard much of Boar either. What I don't get is why they would want Duke's son," Phoenix said.

"Could be any number of reasons. Maybe she can't have kids. Maybe she just wants to hurt Duke. Maybe she's jealous. Maybe this is all

Boar's doing. Don't forget, James is also Reese's son, and there's a history between Boar and Reese's mother," Badger mused.

"I'm going to tear that fucker apart, limb by fucking limb," Carbon growled. I didn't even hear him come in.

"You'll do no such thing until I say you can," Phoenix ordered. "Did you get Reese settled?"

He grinned, "Yeah. Put James in her arms and she turned into a different person. Got to say, I'm damn proud of my little sister. Waterboarding a bitch with ice cold water," he shook his head, and his smile grew. "Didn't know she had it in her."

The brothers laughed at that. Shaker threw in, "You sure you know what you're getting into, Duke?" Their laughter grew louder.

I smiled. "I sure do. I'm damn proud of her, too."

"All right, boys, let's get back to business. I want Reese and James moved to the clubhouse until further notice. We need to find out how that sister got onto the farm property and got to the Martins' house—"

Byte interrupted, "I can answer that. I checked the camera feeds. She pulled up and the gate opened. She had to have a chip in the car to open it, but I can't figure out how she got one."

"Fuck! Can you get that damn system deactivated?"

"Yes. When do you want me to do that?"

"I'm going to send some prospects out there as soon as we're finished. We'll have two on the gate at all times until further notice. I'll have them call you when they get there, and you can deactivate it," Phoenix explained.

"Copper, this shit runs over into your territory. It's not my intention to go around creating problems, but this shit has to be dealt with. You got any thoughts you want to share on how we should go about handling things?"

Copper leaned back in his chair and twiddled his thumbs. "Honestly, we've never had any trouble with the Manglers MC. They keep to their area, and we hardly ever hear anything from them. Boar has contacted me twice over the years to let me know he heard talk of the Disciples of Death MC being in the area. According to Boar, his club has had trouble with them in the past. Anyway, the times I've talked to him, he's seemed like a level-headed guy, so why don't you start by giving him a call and ask about setting up a meeting?"

"You can't be fucking serious?" Carbon

barked, rising to his feet.

"Sit the fuck down," Phoenix ordered. "I know where you're coming from, Carbon. I get it, but maybe Copper has a point. What could it hurt to meet with him and see what he has to say before we go in guns blazing? I promise you will get your turn when and if the time comes."

Carbon dropped back into his chair, silently fuming.

"We'll leave Melissa in the cells for now. I'm going to send two of the prospects to the farm. Duke and Carbon, go get whatever Reese and James will need to stay here for a few weeks. I'm going to go to the hospital to check on Mrs. Martin. I'll give Boar a call in the morning." Phoenix banged the gavel, and we were dismissed.

***

It was damn near three o'clock in the morning when I finally fell into bed beside Reese. I thought she was asleep, but she rolled toward me and placed her hand on my shoulder. "You okay?"

I pulled her into my arms, kissing her temple. "Yeah, sugar. Just tired. It's been a long damn day."

"I know." She moved closer to me and pressed

her lips to mine. She kissed me softly at first. Then, she started kissing along my neck and down my chest. Her lips on my bare chest were driving me crazy. She mumbled against my skin, "Let me make you feel better."

My tired brain didn't register what she meant until her hand wrapped around my shaft, pulling me out of my boxers. Her hot lips surrounded the head of my cock before she took me all the way to the back of her throat. "Oh fuck, sugar," I groaned. She bobbed her head up and down, each pass sucking and licking my cock. It was taking all my willpower not to thrust my hips and fuck her mouth.

She cupped my balls and gently massaged them while she continued working my cock with her glorious mouth. "Come on, Duke, fuck my mouth. I know you want to." Fuck, she didn't have to tell me twice. I grabbed her head and roughly thrust my hips forward. I plunged in and out of her mouth with quick, harsh thrusts. She moaned low and deep. The vibrations were too much for me. "I'm going to come in your dirty little mouth. You better swallow every last drop," I grunted right before I shot my load down her throat. Being the good girl that she was, she did just as I asked and swallowed all of it. Then, she licked me clean.

I flipped her onto her back, shucked her shorts and panties off, and dove face first between her legs. I feasted on her pussy like it was my last meal, devouring her until she came twice. Then, I pulled her into my arms and fell asleep not even a minute later.

CHAPTER TWENTY-THREE

Phoenix

I pulled up to the little hole in the wall bar, Badger and Judge right behind me. Since this was too close to home for my SAA, Copper offered up his own SAA to fill in. Boar agreed to the meeting much easier than I had anticipated. I wasn't sure if that was a good thing or not.

We walked into the bar and spotted Boar and his men right away. We couldn't have missed them since there were only two other patrons in the whole place. Boar stood when we approached the table. "You must be Phoenix." He held out his hand to shake mine. "Nice to finally put a face with the name. I've heard a lot about you over the years."

I shook his hand. "Is that right?" Not expecting an answer, I gestured toward the table. "Shall we?"

He nodded and took a seat. "So, what's this all about?"

I rubbed my chin with my thumb and forefinger, then leaned back in my chair. "We're not here to start trouble, but I'm not going to ease into it either. My brother's son was kidnapped last night by your Old Lady's sister. We caught her on her way to your clubhouse."

Boar pushed back from the table but remained seated. "Fuck, man! Is the kid okay?"

His reaction caught me off guard. I was expecting him to be pissed and immediately go on the defensive, not to be concerned about the kid. "Yeah, kid's fine. I need to know, why was she bringing him to your clubhouse?"

He held his hands out as if that would ward me off. "I don't fucking know. What makes you think she was headed for the clubhouse?"

"A text from your Old Lady telling her to bring him there," I answered pointedly.

Boar turned to the man on his right. "Have a prospect bring Shannon's ass up here right now. Not a word about why." He turned back to face me. "The club had nothing to do with this. We've stayed out of each other's way for years, and I would like to keep it that way."

"And I would like to believe that, but there's a little more to this story. Do you know who that baby's parents are?"

He shook his head. "Not a clue, man. Should I?"

I schooled my expression and told him, "The baby's mother is Tank's daughter and the father is your Old Lady's husband."

Boar jumped to his feet, causing everyone at the table to stand, both SAA's reaching for their guns. Boar cursed and then realized the tension he had created. "Calm down, boys. I'm just fucking pissed is all."

"You didn't know she was married?" I carefully asked.

"Fuck no. Who the hell is she married to?"

I cleared my throat, "My SAA, Duke, also known as John Jackson."

He turned his angry eyes toward Judge. Judge just smirked and said, "We ain't that stupid. I'm the Devil Springs SAA, filling in for my cousin today. Name's Judge by the way."

Boar dropped back into his chair and leaned forward, elbows on the table. "You said the baby's mother is Tank's daughter?" I nodded.

"This being Reese, my son's ex-girlfriend?" I nodded again. "I see. All roads led to me, and here you are."

"That about sums it up."

A woman walked through the front door and made her way straight to Boar. "Honey, is everything okay? They said I needed to come here but wouldn't tell me why." So this was Shannon.

Boar pointed to a chair. "Sit down." She did, and her eyes widened in fear. "Got anything you want to tell me about your sister?"

She dropped her eyes to the floor and sucked in a sharp breath. "What has she done now?"

"I think you know what she did," Boar barked.

"Last night, she said she had taken John's baby. I told her to bring the baby to the clubhouse. I didn't believe her at first. Then, I thought if I could get her to bring the baby to me, we could get him back to John. She never showed up, and she stopped answering my calls and texts, so I thought this was one of her usual shenanigans," she explained through her tears.

"That's a good start," Boar snapped. "Now, you want to tell me who the fuck John is?"

She wrapped her arms around herself and sniffled. "He's my husband. I'm sorry I never told you. I haven't seen him in 10 years. We weren't married for very long, but I never did anything about the marriage. I'm so sorry," she wailed.

"Shannon, I'm going to ask you this one time, and you better give me the damn truth or these men right here just might kill us all before it's over with, you hear me?" She sat up straighter in her chair and rapidly nodded her head. "Did you arrange the kidnapping or have anything to do with it?"

She shook her head. "No! I would never do anything like that. I didn't know until after the fact. I didn't even know John had a baby until last night. You know she says crazy shit all the time, but she's never actually done anything."

"That you know of," Boar added.

I studied the woman sitting before me. She appeared to be giving honest answers, and her tears seemed genuine. Damn, part of me wished Carbon was with us; he was far more skilled at reading people than I was. "Where is your sister now?"

She turned her head and seemed to notice me and the two men beside me for the first time. She looked back to Boar, unsure if she should answer me. "You answer any questions they have with absolute honesty," Boar ordered.

"I don't know where she is. After I told her to

217

bring me the baby, she stopped taking my calls. Wait. Are you here because—? Did she—? Please tell me she didn't."

I hoped I wasn't making a mistake, but I believed that she didn't know anything about the kidnapping. "She did."

She crumpled over, her body shaking with violent sobs. She said something, but I couldn't make out what it was with the way she was carrying on. Boar had no sympathy for her, though I can't say I blamed him. "Don't ask me. You ask them," he barked.

She lifted her tear-stained face. "Is the baby okay?"

"He's fine. He's been returned to his parents," I said. I quirked a brow, "You don't want to know about your sister?"

She wiped the tears from her face and resolutely said, "No, I don't. She's been nothing but a pain in my ass for years, always causing trouble, threatening to pull some stupid stunt like this. She got herself into this, and she can get herself out of it as far as I'm concerned."

Boar tugged on her hand and pulled her to her feet. "Go back to the clubhouse with the prospect. We have some other shit to discuss when I get back." He turned to face me. "Unless you need her for anything else?"

"Nope. The rest we can discuss with you."

Shannon quickly exited the bar. Boar sat down with a sigh, "I know this looks bad, but she's telling the truth about Melissa. Shannon's said before that she's always had problems. I've only known her for a few years, and during that time, she's been nothing but trouble. Honestly, I can't say I'm sad to see her shit finally caught up with her. Is there anything we can do to smooth this over?"

"The way I see it, it wasn't your doing, so there's nothing to smooth over, but maybe you'd be willing to help us out by answering some other questions."

"Depends on what those questions are, but I'll answer if I can do so without endangering myself or my club," he carefully stated.

"Where's your son?" I bluntly asked.

His face contorted with disgust. "Who the fuck knows. That boy is a disgrace. I kicked his ass out of my house and out of my club almost two years ago. I ain't seen or heard from him since."

I couldn't hide my surprise at his answer. "No shit. You mind if I ask why?"

He grunted. "Not something I like to discuss, but as a show of good faith, I'll tell you. About two weeks after he was patched in, he beat up one of the club girls and tried to force himself on her. One of the other girls came to get me, told me she heard her friend screaming behind a locked door. I got there in time to stop him from raping her, but I have no doubt that he would have had he not been interrupted. I don't condone raping and beating women. He was stripped of his cut, beat within an inch of his life, and sent packing."

That was interesting coming from him, especially after everything Carbon said about him and his club. Boar interrupted my thoughts, "I know what you're thinking. You wouldn't expect that coming from me because you've probably heard that I was behind the murder of Tank and his family." He looked down at his lap and lowered his voice, "I loved Heather, but it wasn't a healthy love. She came along right after my mom died, and I latched onto her. When she left me, I tried to stop her and lost my head for a bit. It was like losing my mom all over again. I'm not proud of it, but I can admit that I crossed some lines I shouldn't have crossed where she was concerned. I never did anything to hurt her. Later on, I recognized our relationship for what it was, an unhealthy attachment on my part. She moved on, I moved on, and that was that. Still, it cut me deeply when I learned of her death. I was hell-bent on finding out who did it, but when the fingers started pointing in my direction, I thought it was best to keep out of the limelight."

"You think it was a setup?" I asked.

"I've always thought that, and I've carried that guilt with me every day since it happened," he told me.

I knocked my knuckles twice on the table. "I think that about wraps it up for us. Thank you for coming out and answering our questions."

"No problem. Thanks for bringing some things to my attention. Your boy will be getting divorce papers soon. Should I have them sent to the clubhouse?"

I smiled. "Please do. He's been trying to find Shannon's whereabouts so he could send some to her."

"Oh, well if he already has some drawn up, send them to my clubhouse. I'll make sure she signs and returns them," he said.

We shook hands and left the bar. I stopped beside my bike and took a deep, cleansing breath. That did not go how I expected, at all.

CHAPTER TWENTY-FOUR

Duke

I was about to lose my mind waiting for Phoenix to get back from his meeting with Boar. I had so much pent-up rage and nowhere to direct it. I hoped like hell Phoenix came back with answers.

"You want to get in the ring, brother?" Carbon asked.

"With you? Hell no. You're just as keyed up as I am, and that won't end well, especially for me."

He laughed. "Yeah, you're probably right about that. Hey, where's your sister?"

"She's with Ember and Reese. Why?" I asked. He better not be making a play for my sister.

"Just curious. Didn't know if she went back

home, or if she was staying around for a while," he shrugged, seeming casual, but I wasn't sure I was buying it.

"She's staying for a bit. She wants to spend some time with James," I said, eyeing him curiously.

"Where's she staying?"

"Why?" I asked, defensively. He had no reason to be asking anything about my sister.

"What is your deal? I'm just trying to have a conversation with you." He chuckled. "Oh, you think I'm after your sister?"

"I don't know, are you?"

"So, you can get with my sister behind my back and knock her up, but your sister is off limits?" he spat.

"Will you two knock that shit off? I swear, every time I turn around the two of you are bickering like little children," Phoenix shouted. "Now get your asses up and get to Church."

When everyone had arrived, Phoenix filled us in on his meeting with Boar. I couldn't believe what Phoenix was saying. Shannon had nothing to do with having my son kidnapped, and it was all her little sister's doing? Was she also the one who ran Reese off the road? What about the letters, who had sent those? I just couldn't wrap my mind around any of it. It made more sense for the culprit to be Shannon, not Melissa.

Carbon's outraged bellow brought me back to the present. "And you seriously believe that lying sack of shit? Of course, he denied it and fed you a good story, he's had nine years to come up with it." Carbon's face was red, and he was pacing the back of the room. He looked like a bull ready to charge.

"I'm going to let that slide because I know how hard this topic is for you, but consider that your one and only warning. I will not tolerate disrespect from you or anyone else. Now sit your ass down and listen to the rest of what I have to say," Phoenix ordered.

Carbon grunted, blew out a long breath, and hesitantly returned to his seat. Phoenix continued sharing the details of the discussion he had with Boar and his men. "What do we know about the Disciples of Death MC?" Phoenix asked.

Heads shook and a few murmured something along the lines of "not much." Shaker leaned back in his chair and crossed his arms over his chest. "I'm sorry, Phoenix, but I'm kind of leaning toward Carbon on this one. He's had plenty of time to come up with a good story. If the Disciples of Death had enough of an issue with our club or Boar's to kill a brother and his family, don't you think we would have heard more from them over the years?"

"No, I don't. We moved, remember?" Phoenix asked flatly. He had a point. Right after Boar became president of the Manglers and Carbon's family was killed, Phoenix became the president of Blackwings and moved the club to Croftridge.

"Right, but it still doesn't make any sense," Shaker continued. "Let's say they did kill Carbon's family to try to pin it on Boar. They left absolutely no evidence indicating the Manglers were responsible, which is like rule number one in trying to set someone up. On top of that, they just let it go when their plan didn't work out? Why go to all the trouble of killing four people and then say, 'That didn't work out like I thought, so I guess I'll just give up.'?"

Phoenix cleared his throat. "Let me clarify what I am saying and what I'm not saying. I'm not saying the Manglers didn't kill Carbon's parents and I'm not saying the Disciples of Death did. What I am saying is I believe Boar didn't do it, didn't order it, and knew nothing about it."

"You think someone in his club did it?" Shaker asked.

Phoenix sighed. "I have no fucking clue who

did it. Don't misunderstand me, I want to know and hold them accountable for murdering our brother, his Old Lady, and two of their children in cold blood, but that was nine years ago. There were no leads back then, and this new information is all speculation. We need to focus on the things happening right now and get that shit handled before it escalates any further."

Carbon asked, "Do we know if the bitch downstairs is the one who ran my sister off the road and tried to kill her?"

Phoenix shook his head. "No, I don't know that. I plan to question her again as soon as Byte is finished going through her phone. Where are you on that, Byte?"

Byte looked up, said phone in his hand. "Almost finished. Found some things of interest, but nothing indicating she was the one who hit Reese or sent the letters. I haven't had a chance to do a full search on her yet, but I can get started on that ASAP, assuming it's okay to drop the searches on Shannon and Boar."

"Yeah, put them on the backburner for now and see what you can find on Melissa. What things of interest did you find on her phone?"

"Her texts with her sister are sporadic, and it does look like she only texts her when she's causing trouble, which is consistent with Shannon's story. She does text someone she has saved as Nemo frequently. I'll run a trace on the number and see if it gives me anything. They communicate frequently, but I can't figure out what they're saying to each other. It's like a foreign language, but not one I've ever seen," Byte told us.

"Has this Nemo person tried to contact her since we've had her?" Phoenix asked.

Byte shook his head. "No, it looks like she sent a text to him right before we caught up with her last night. Don't have a clue what it says though."

"Let's see it," Phoenix said. Byte handed him the phone. Phoenix studied it for a few moments then passed it off to Badger. The phone passed from brother to brother until it made it to my hands. I looked down at the screen.

Nemo: Esu puuj foarzg.

I blinked twice to make sure I was seeing what I thought I was seeing. What the fuck did that mean? I looked down at it once more and passed the phone to the next brother. It continued around the room until it made it back around to Phoenix. He looked at it once more and handed it back to Byte. "Anybody got any idea what that says?"

Not a one of us did. This bitch was apparently an all new level of crazy, complete with her own damn language.

"Duke," Phoenix called out, "has Reese gotten any more threatening letters?"

"Not that I know of. I haven't checked the PO Box recently, but they weren't coming through regular mail anyway. I'll stop by the post office this afternoon and check."

"Let me know one way or the other. For now, everyone stay alert and aware of your surroundings. Reese and James are to stay at the clubhouse and not leave the property, even with protection. Byte you keep digging and doing your thing. We'll reconvene when we have something new or at the next scheduled Church, whichever comes first."

***

I stopped by my room to check on Reese and James, but found it empty. After searching the clubhouse and still not finding them, I started to worry. She knew she wasn't supposed to leave the clubhouse grounds. She might not follow the rules if it was just her, but she would never knowingly put our son in danger, so where in the hell were they?

I pushed the back door open with more force than necessary, causing it to slam against the side of the building. All heads turned toward me, including Reese's and James's. They were in the pool with Ember and Harper. Dash, Carbon, and Shaker were sitting in chairs along the side.

"Duke, you scared me. Is everything okay?" Reese asked, eyes wide.

I inhaled slowly, trying to calm myself. "Yeah, everything is fine. Just didn't know where you guys were."

"Oh, sorry. We decided to go swimming while you guys were in Church. Do you want to join us?" She smiled sweetly at me.

I really would love to jump in the pool with my family. My. Family. But I couldn't. "I would love to, sugar, but I have to run by the post office and take care of a few other things. You need anything while I'm out?"

"No, I'm good right now. Will you be long?"

"I'll try not to be." She made her way over to the side of the pool, pushing James in a little baby float. I squatted down to kiss the top of his head. Then, I kissed my girl. "Be good, sugar."

"I will. Just until you get back." The little minx

winked and swam off.

CHAPTER TWENTY-FIVE

Reese

Duke returned several hours later, and he didn't seem to be in a great mood. "You okay?" I asked.

He sighed and sat down on the bed. "Yeah, I'm just tired, and frustrated."

"What's got you so frustrated?"

He grunted. "Club business. Sorry, sugar." I really hated it when he said that. They all did it. Like us women were too stupid to figure out what was going on by ourselves.

"So, this has nothing to do with the fact that your wife's sister kidnapped our son and you don't know why? Or that you also don't know who was sending me the letters or who ran me off the road?" I asked, with one eyebrow arched.

"Should've known you'd figure out what was going on without me telling you," he grumbled.

"What can I do to help?" I asked, moving to straddle his lap and circle my arms around his neck.

He placed a soft kiss on my cheek and pulled me closer to him. "Nothing, sugar. Just keep to the clubhouse and stay out of trouble until we've got this sorted. Need you and my boy safe."

"I can do that," I promised. "You sure there's nothing else I can do?" I asked as I kissed along his jawline and rocked my hips against him.

His hands gripped my hips and held me in place. "Where's James?"

"Spending some time with his Aunt Harper and Uncle Carbon," I said, straining to get closer to him.

Duke growled and reversed our positions, coming down on top of me on the bed. He yanked my shirt up and pulled the cups of my bra down. "Fuck, Reese, I love your tits," he said while palming and squeezing both globes with his hands.

"And you have the prettiest pink nipples," he added while rolling each hardened peak between his fingers.

I arched my back and moaned, "Duke."

He grabbed my wrists and raised them above my head, holding both in place with one hand. Grinning down at me, he asked, "Can you keep them above your head on your own?"

Well, of course I could, but who would want to? I smirked. "I can, but I probably won't."

His grin grew even wider. "I was hoping you'd say that." He unbuckled his belt and pulled it from his jeans. Leaning forward, he wrapped the belt around both of my wrists and secured it to the headboard.

Once he was satisfied with his makeshift restraint, he quickly stripped us both and climbed back onto the bed on his knees beside my head. Taking his cock in his hand, he stroked it a few times before he said, "Open."

I readily complied and sucked the head of his cock into my mouth. "Fuck," he hissed. I sucked harder and lifted my head to take as much of him as I could. I repeatedly pulled back and moved forward, at a slow pace, just to tease him.

"That's not going to work, sugar." He moved to the end of the bed and climbed up between my legs. "Let's see how you like being teased." With that, he latched onto my clit and started sucking. He would bring me to the brink of release and stop. He did this three times before I lost my patience.

I writhed on the bed, yanking against my restraints and raising my hips in a futile attempt to get closer to him. He grinned up at me. "What is it, baby?"

"You know damn well what it is! Stop fucking with me and let me come."

"You want me to stop fucking with you?"

"Yes! I mean, no. Damn it, Duke. I want you to fuck me."

"Well, all you had to do was say so, sugar." He climbed up my body and lined himself up at my entrance. "You want it hard or soft, sugar?"

"Show me what you got, biker boy."

He plunged into me with one thrust and proceeded to fuck me with a ferocity I didn't know he was capable of. I seriously began to worry about the integrity of his mattress. That thought quickly vanished when he flipped me over, pulled my hips up, and pushed into me from behind.

From this new angle, he was hitting that spot deep inside of me that would send me over the edge in a matter of seconds. "Oh, Duke, I'm going to come."

"Yeah, you fucking are," he grunted as he

picked up his pace.

And I did. I came so hard I didn't even realize he had finished as well for longer than I care to admit. When I did return to reality, Duke had freed my hands and had me tucked into his side while he caught his breath.

"You okay, sugar?"

"Fuck, yes. Now, I need you to wash me off in the shower."

And wash me off he did. Three times, actually. Because he made a mess the first two times.

CHAPTER TWENTY-SIX

Reese

For the next week, I did exactly as I promised. I stayed at the clubhouse, let an officer know if I was going outside, and stayed out of trouble. But enough was enough. A week had gone by and from what I could tell, they didn't have anything new. I overheard Byte talking about some secret code language, but he spotted me in the hallway and stopped talking before I could hear anything useful.

I was beginning to lose my patience with the whole thing. I had been confined to basically a bedroom for six weeks after the wreck. The day I was given the okay to walk again, I was locked down at the clubhouse. I knew they would eventually get to the bottom of things, but they weren't doing it fast enough for me. So, I decided to take matters into my own hands.

Knowing Ember was a shit liar, I asked her if she would watch James while I helped Harper color her hair. She readily agreed, understanding that I didn't want James around all of those fumes. Next, I found Harper and asked her if she would be willing to help me with something that we would eventually be caught for and would most definitely piss off the brothers. Lucky for me, Harper had a little bad girl in her and was more than happy to help out.

I got James settled with Ember and made sure the coast was clear. Most of the brothers were at the garage or out at the farm. Ranger was at the bar, possibly sleeping, and two of the prospects were playing video games in the common room. Harper and I tiptoed past the bar and down the hallway, coming to a stop in front of the door that led downstairs to the cells.

"You keep watch and let me know if anyone is coming. I just need a minute or two to get this lock open," I told her while pulling out my lock picking set.

She grinned. "Nice. Will you teach me how to do that sometime?"

"Hell, yeah. I think you've just officially become my partner in crime," I chuckled. I got to work on the lock, and not even a minute later we were quietly closing the door behind us. I turned back to Harper. "You know what's down here, right?"

She rolled her eyes. "Yeah, it's like their little jail or something. I assume we're going to see the girl who took James, right?"

Surprised by her knowledge, I stumbled over my words, "Uh, yeah, that's right." We continued down the stairs and made our way to the cell that contained Melissa.

Harper gasped when she saw her. "You!" she screamed, pointing an accusing finger at the bitch. "You did this shit?"

"You know her?" I asked.

Harper chuckled darkly. "Yes, I know her. She's Shannon's sister, but more than that, she's the bitch who made my life hell until we moved away. What is your fucking problem with my family?"

Melissa sat up on the bed and looked at her fingernails. "I didn't have a problem with your family, Harper. It was just you. You know how much I like John." She looked up and smiled cruelly.

Harper turned toward me and winked. I had

no idea why she did that. She stepped forward and tapped her chin with her index finger. "Oh, that's right, you have a thing for Duke, have for years. But he never wanted you, did he?" Melissa's face started to redden.

"He even told you that, several times, if I remember correctly. Then, he up and married your sister. Your. Sister. It must suck to be that not wanted."

Melissa jumped off the bed and flew to the bars of the cell. She wrapped her fingers around the bars and started shaking them as she screamed. "You shut your fucking mouth! You don't know what you're talking about. He did want me. He had to marry my sister because I wasn't old enough. If you weren't stupid enough to get yourself kidnapped, he would have married me when I turned 18. But nooooo! He had to save your ass, so he married Shannon. Then, you took him away from Arizona. Away from me. And now I have to contend with this bitch," she pointed a finger at me and snarled.

Harper placed her hands on her hips and casually said, "You think I'm the reason he's not with you? He didn't stay here for me. Hell, we don't even live in the same state now as it is. He just didn't want to come back for you. He didn't want you then and he doesn't want you now. What? Did you really think kidnapping his son would make him want to be with you?"

"No!" she screamed. "I wanted him to think Shannon did it so he would finally divorce her and marry me! And having his baby and then refusing to fucking die! What is with you people? No one is working with me on this. But that's okay," she cackled, "that's why I always have a backup plan."

"Enlighten us, oh crazy cunt, what is your grand backup plan?" Harper asked flatly.

Melissa smiled knowingly. "Nemo."

"Nemo?" Harper and I asked at the same time.

Still smiling, she nodded and sang, "Nemo's coming." She kept singing it over and over and over.

Suddenly, another voice interrupted us, a voice that was decidedly unfamiliar. "I can't take this anymore. Reverse it so she'll shut up. That's all you need to do!"

I froze, as did Harper. She leaned closer to me and whispered, "Where in the fuck did that come from?"

"I'm in the cell over here, you twits," the voice said. They had another prisoner down here? Who the hell was this?

I shakily asked, "And you are?"

He scoffed. "Like you don't know."

Harper and I inched closer to his cell, all the while the bitch was still singing about Nemo coming. When we got close enough to see inside the cell, I almost lost the contents of my stomach. A severely malnourished man with overgrown facial hair was sitting in the corner of the cell, covered from head to toe in bruises, blood, and general filth. He was holding one arm against his chest, and it appeared to be at an odd angle. I croaked, "I really don't."

He scoffed again, "I'm Octavius Jones."

I stumbled back and fell on my ass, taking Harper down with me. I wanted to scream, but I couldn't seem to get any air into my lungs. We needed to get out of there, immediately. I thought he was dead. They said he died over a year ago, that he killed himself. He'd been here the whole time? Realization brutally slammed into me. That's why Duke stopped on the stairs the other night, so he could make sure I wouldn't see Octavius. "We need to get out of here, Harper. Now!"

"Okay, okay. Let's go." She stood and reached out to give me a hand. Once I was on my feet, we wasted no time sprinting up the stairs. When we reached the top, the door swung open, and we were met with three furious bikers. Duke, Carbon, and Phoenix. Fucking A, man.

CHAPTER TWENTY-SEVEN

Duke

When I got back to the clubhouse, I found Ember in our room with James. She explained that Reese was helping Harper dye her hair and didn't want the baby around the fumes. I checked everywhere I could think of, but couldn't find the girls anywhere. The more I looked, the more suspicious I became. Harper wasn't one to make sudden or drastic changes to her hair.

I found Carbon in the common room and asked if he knew where the girls were. He didn't, but got up to help me look. By this time, we had attracted Phoenix's attention, and he joined our search party. We walked down the back hallway to check, even though they had no business being back that way.

I think I noticed it first. "Motherfucker," I cursed and pointed at what I saw. The damn door to the underground cells was slightly ajar. "You don't think they went down there do you?"

Carbon stomped ahead. "Have you met Reese? Of course she went down there. Harper, too." I could see Reese doing something like that, but not Harper. She was too timid to be doing things like breaking rules and confronting dangerous criminals.

As soon as we reached the door, it swung open, revealing two frantic and terrified girls. "What the fuck do you think you're doing?" I roared at both of them.

"Me?" Reese shrieked. "Me? You're the one that has a living corpse down there! Now unless you want me to vomit all over your pants and shoes, get the fuck out of my way." She shoved her way through the three of us and ran toward our room like her ass was on fire, Harper not even two steps behind her.

"Oh, hell no. The second she's finished puking, she's talking," I stated, stomping my way down the hall behind them.

We followed them into my room, and Reese

emerged from the bathroom a few minutes later, looking quite green. That's what she got for doing things she knew she had no business doing. I didn't feel a bit sorry for her.

Ember was sitting on the bed with James in her arms looking back and forth between the two very clearly divided parties in the room. "Should I take James out to the common room or maybe to Dash's room?" she hesitantly asked.

"Do you mind taking him to Dash's room for a few minutes?" Reese asked. "Duke or I will come to get him soon."

Once they were gone, Phoenix started, "Just what in the hell did the two of you think you were doing?"

Reese took the lead. Brave little shit that she was, stood tall and said, "I'm sorry for picking the lock and going down to the cells, but I'm not going to apologize for trying to speed this along. I want this over just as much as everyone else does. So, I went downstairs to have a chat with Melissa."

"You had no right to do that!" Phoenix roared.

"Let's call a spade a spade, all right? You aren't really all that pissed off about me being down there to talk to her, because you've already let me have a go at her in the basement. What you're really pissed off about is what else I saw while I was there, am I right?" Reese asked, voice steadier than I would have thought possible.

"No, I'm pissed off because you showed blatant disrespect for me and my club by going down there without permission."

Reese swallowed, but kept her eyes on Phoenix. "To be fair, Phoenix, you never told me I wasn't allowed to go down to the cells. You said I had to stay in the clubhouse and ask an officer to accompany me if I wanted to go outside. You didn't mention that certain parts of the clubhouse were off limits."

Phoenix's jaw clenched. "The locked door should have tipped you off."

"Not really, I've been picking locks since I was a child. People lock doors out of habit, by mistake, to keep people in, for all kinds of reasons other than keeping someone out," Reese explained, continuing to defend her position.

"You should probably stop now, Reese," Carbon advised, nodding to Phoenix who was getting angrier by the second.

"Okay, fine," she huffed. "While technically, I'm right that you didn't say it was off limits, I did know that I wasn't meant to be in the basement. I didn't do it out of disrespect or anything like that. I was just trying to help. I knew she couldn't hurt me, and I honestly had no idea you still had Octavius as a prisoner."

"Who said that was Octavius?" Phoenix demanded.

Reese and Harper answered at the same time, "He did."

"You talked to him?" Phoenix yelled.

"Not exactly. He talked to us. He wanted us to make Melissa shut up. She was saying the same thing over and over; then, Octavius said the weirdest thing before he told us his name."

"What did he say?" Phoenix asked, anxiously, no doubt hoping it had something to do with Annabelle.

"He said to make her shut up we needed to reverse it. Do you know what he meant by that?" Reese asked.

Phoenix shook his head. "What was she saying?"

Harper huffed and jumped in, "Oh, she had a lot to say. She told us all about her obsession with Duke and why she kidnapped James. Oh, and that she was the one who hit Reese. Then, she started singing 'Nemo's coming' over and over and over. I agree with the skinny dude, it was maddening."

"Motherfucker!" Carbon said at the same time Reese muttered, "Son of a bitch."

"What?" the rest of us asked.

"Omen," they said in unison. "Nemo is Omen."

***

After Harper and Reese filled us in on everything Melissa said, Phoenix called us into Church. When everyone was up-to-speed, we began discussing our next steps.

Phoenix directed his gaze to Carbon. "Carbon, I know how you feel about this, and, for right now, I'm willing to explore other avenues first, but I really think we should talk to Boar again. Omen is his son, and, even though he's disowned him, he might be able to help us find him. Don't forget, Boar's Old Lady is the crazy bitch's sister. She might be able to help us find him, too."

Carbon nodded. "I don't like it, but my parents and siblings have been dead nine years, and my sister is still alive and in danger. If bringing him in will put a stop to that, then it would be foolish of me to say no."

"I'm going to see if he'd be willing to come here to the clubhouse, maybe have a chat with our newest prisoner. Everyone okay with that?"

Phoenix asked.

Heads nodded in agreement. "Carbon, if you don't think you can maintain your composure, you don't have to see him. I won't hold that against you, though I think you should talk to the man. Out of all of us, you're by far the most skilled at reading people."

Carbon grunted. "Let's see if he agrees to come, first. Then, I'll see where my head's at when he shows up."

"All right, I'll give Boar a call and see if he's willing to help us out. Duke, you have a problem if he wants to bring his Old Lady with him?"

"Not at all, Prez." I'm not sure how Reese would feel about it, but Shannon being at the clubhouse wouldn't make a bit of difference to me. I never had feelings for her, and I would venture to say that she never had feelings for me either. As an added bonus, it would give me the perfect opportunity to get the divorce papers from her. "If she comes with Boar, have her bring those papers we sent last week."

"I'll pass that along. All right, brothers, I'll let you know when I know."

CHAPTER TWENTY-EIGHT

Duke

Boar agreed to come down to our clubhouse the next morning. He didn't want to bring Shannon with him, even though she wanted to come. Phoenix assured him that she would be completely safe here. He finally agreed to let her come when Phoenix said his VP and SAA could come with him.

Reese knew that Shannon was coming along. She said she was fine with it, but I wasn't so sure she was telling the truth. She also knew that Shannon would be allowed downstairs if needed, while she would not be allowed to visit Melissa again. I knew this would be a problem no matter what she said.

They showed up a little after lunchtime. The prospect called up from the gate to let Phoenix know they had arrived. Moments later, three sharp knocks sounded from the front doors.

Phoenix shot a look of warning to everyone in the room before he pulled the front doors open wide. "Boar, thanks for coming. Come on in," he gestured to the large common room. "Care for something to drink?"

"I'd love a beer. I'm sure the boys would, too. Shan, you want a water?"

"Please," she quietly said. She didn't look like the same girl I knew years ago. She had grown into her features, her hair was lighter and a lot longer, but it was the overall lack of menace that really changed the way she looked. Her eyes didn't hold the same undertone of malevolence like they once did. She seemed to be happy, and it looked good on her.

Her eyes finally landed on me. She softly smiled. "Hi, John." She cleared her throat and fidgeted with her hands, "It's been a long time."

"Yeah, it has…" I trailed off. What was there to say? I had absolutely nothing.

After a few beats of awkward silence, she said, "I brought the papers for you." She reached into the bag she had strapped across her chest and shuffled some things around. She pulled out a stack of papers and handed them to me. "All signed and initialed. Can you send me a final copy or whatever when it has been filed?"

"No problem. Thanks for bringing these with you," I said. I glanced around the room. Just as I thought, every single person was watching us. The thought of everyone's eyes on me made me so uncomfortable it was making it hard for me to talk to her.

I felt a small hand on my arm. Just like that, everything felt right again. I looked down at Reese and smiled widely at her. "Hey, sugar." I leaned down to give her a quick kiss, wanting her to know I had nothing to hide in front of Shannon, or anyone for that matter. "Reese, this is Shannon. Shannon, this is my girlfriend, Reese, and this is our son, James."

Shannon smiled. "Hello, Reese. I'm sure you probably aren't thrilled to meet me, and I completely understand that. I want you to know that I'm sorry for what my sister has done to you," she gestured to Reese's still booted foot, "and I'm so glad your son was returned to you safe and sound."

Reese stood taller, "You're right, I wasn't

thrilled about you coming here, but you arrived with signed divorce papers. That's a good way to sway the jury in your favor." Reese paused and looked down at her foot, "You don't need to apologize for your sister. From what I know, it wasn't your doing."

Boar interrupted, "Shan, are you okay to stay here with Reese and the other girls while we go discuss a few things?" She nodded. "Do you want one of the boys to stay out here with you?"

"No, babe, I think I'll be okay. Go do what you need to do. I'll wait right here." She leaned in and gave him a soft kiss. They seemed to genuinely care for one another. Not at all what I expected when I first learned that her and Boar were together.

We left the girls in the common room and went into the room we used for Church. Phoenix didn't tell Boar very much over the phone. Once he had been filled in on all the details, Boar asked, "So, you want me to help you find my son?"

Phoenix nodded, "That and anything you could shed light on would be appreciated. Reese has gotten Melissa to shout out a few things in anger, which is how we learned about her connection with Omen. I know it's a lot to ask."

Boar looked around the room, seeming to

pause for a brief moment when his eyes landed on Carbon before continuing. "I don't mind helping in any way I can. That boy is a disgrace. I haven't considered him my son for a long time now. Some of the things he has done—" he shook his head. "I didn't raise him like that. I don't know where it comes from or why he is the way he is. I tried everything I could think of to change his ways, but nothing worked. Finally, I just had to wash my hands of him."

Carbon was silently taking this all in. Studying every move Boar made, analyzing every word he said. Boar must have felt his scrutinizing gaze. He raised his head and looked directly at Carbon. He softly said, "You must be Heather's boy. You're built like your father, but you've got her eyes."

Carbon nodded, but I noticed his jaw clench and his fists tighten in his lap. Phoenix noticed, too, and quickly redirected the focus of the conversation. "You likely won't be able to help us with this, but it's a good starting point." Phoenix pulled out Melissa's cell phone and opened her text thread with Nemo/Omen. "You have any idea what language this is?"

Boar nodded. "I know what it is, but it's not a language, not like you're thinking. Shannon's told me on several occasions that Melissa was constantly making up her own languages and codes for words, so she could communicate without anyone else knowing what she was saying. Shannon liked to point out how she couldn't communicate with anyone if no one else knew the language. Anyway, I'd guess that's one of Melissa's made up languages, but I have no idea what it says."

"Would Shannon know?" I asked.

He shrugged. "I'm not sure. Call her to the door, and we'll ask her."

Shannon stopped at the doorway. Boar showed her the text message and asked if she thought it was one of Melissa's languages. When she said she did, Boar then asked if she knew how to read any of it. "Not really, but from what I've heard her say about it over the years, it's like those little puzzles in the newspapers, where they mix up the alphabet and you have to figure out which letter is which."

"Thanks, babe. Go on back out there. Shouldn't be much longer," Boar told her, kissing her cheek.

Byte leaned forward to take the phone back. "Is she saying this is just a cryptogram?"

"A what?" Phoenix asked.

"Never mind," Byte grumbled. "I should have this deciphered soon."

"Should we wait for you to do that before we continue?" Phoenix asked.

"Probably," Byte said, already scribbling notes on a piece of paper. "Might answer some questions."

Not even five minutes later, Byte had deciphered the secret code and translated the text messages between Melissa and Nemo/Omen.

Boar sat back in his chair and looked to the ceiling. He took in a large breath and blew it out slowly. "I know you don't need my permission to go after my son, but you have it. I stripped him of his patch, so this has nothing to do with my club. As far as I'm concerned, this is just another piece of scum getting his dues."

Phoenix shot Boar a skeptical look. "It ain't my business, but that seems awfully harsh for beating up and almost raping a club girl. Did something else happen?"

Boar looked down at his hands. "Nothing that I could prove, though I wish like hell I could have. I would've turned him in or killed him myself."

Phoenix sat quietly for a few moments. "Anything you want to share with us?"

Boar looked across the room at Carbon then back to Phoenix. Boar subtly moved his head in Carbon's direction while keeping his eyes on Phoenix. Not subtle enough though. Carbon saw it and was on his feet in a flash. "You mean your piece of shit offspring killed my family?" he roared.

"Badger, take over. Shaker, Duke, you're with me," Phoenix barked, already moving toward the raging behemoth. Phoenix got him in a rear naked choke hold and forced him to his knees, while Shaker and I stood on either side ready to pounce. "Lock it down, Carbon," Phoenix demanded. Carbon's body stiffened. He wasn't fighting anymore, but he wasn't letting it go either.

"Duke, get Reese in here now," Shaker said. Phoenix nodded his assent.

I went out to get Reese, only to find that she had taken James into the restroom to change his diaper. What happened next blew me away. My little sister silently rose to her feet and walked toward the Church door. She walked in without preamble, me hot on her heels. Harper went straight to Carbon and placed her tiny little hands on his cheeks. She leaned in and put her mouth so close to his ear I couldn't make out what she said to him. Whatever it was, his body relaxed, and he dropped his head, keeping his eyes on the ground. Harper said something else to him, patted his shoulder, and left the room, throwing, "You're welcome," over her shoulder.

Carbon cleared his throat. "I'm good, Prez."

"You sure? I'm not doing that shit again today," Phoenix griped.

"I'm sure. Carry on. I'm just going to sit back here." Carbon dropped into a chair by the door, which I found to be extremely odd.

Boar eyed Carbon warily, but began speaking again. "I wasn't referring to Heather and her family, but I do think my son killed your grandmother. I have no actual proof, but certain things he said and did around that time led me to believe he was responsible for her death. It wasn't long after that when I found out about him roughing up Reese, and then I caught him trying to rape one of the club girls. To top it off, I'm fairly certain he was the one who killed my father."

Carbon sat forward in his chair. "My grandmother wasn't murdered. She died of a heart attack."

Boar looked directly at Carbon. "Yeah, and every one of us in this room knows how to make certain things appear different than they really are." His shoulders sagged. The man appeared to be carrying the weight of the world on his shoulders, but he forged on. "Like I said, I don't have any proof other than odd comments he made at the time. He did the same sort of thing around the time my father died."

"Why are you bringing this up? You have no proof, it's not like anything can be done about it," Carbon asked with no animosity in his tone. Maybe Harper really had brought him back from the brink.

"I just wanted you all to know that I'm not blind to what my son is. He's always had a barely contained hatred for me, and I've never known why. I thought things were changing when he wanted to prospect, but now I believe he was just trying to use the club as a way to take me out. He's beyond help and needs to be put down before he can ruin any more lives. I'll do anything I can to help you catch him. I prefer not to be the one who ends his life, but I will if I have to," Boar said solemnly.

Phoenix clapped Boar on the shoulder. "Thanks, man. We'd appreciate any help we can get."

Boar nodded and straightened, seeming to

gather his strength to move on. He looked in Byte's direction. "Did you get anything from those text messages?"

Byte cleared his throat, "Not sure. The last one she sent said 'I've been caught.' Prior to that, there's not much other than them saying things like 'I'll be there in 5' or 'See you back at HQ.' Nothing that gives away a location or what they were planning to do next."

"Did you say HQ?" Boar asked.

"Yeah, they mention HQ several times. That mean something?" Byte asked.

"Maybe. There was this little ramshackle cabin out in the middle of the woods, not far from Devil Springs, that he liked to play in when he was younger. He found it when we were out for a father-son fishing and hunting trip. He used to call it his headquarters. He drove me fucking nuts asking me to go fishing or hunting all the damn time just so he could go play in that cabin. The thing had been long abandoned when we found it. Never gave much thought to where he went when I told him to leave, but it would make sense for him to go there," Boar told us.

"Can you point it out on a map?" Phoenix asked.

"Yeah, the general area anyway."

Byte already had a map of Devil Springs and the surrounding area pulled up on his laptop. Boar leaned closer to the screen and pointed to where he thought the place was. Byte did some shit with his computer, and suddenly we were all looking at a satellite image of the most run-down cabin I had ever seen.

"That's it," Boar said. "Shall we go see if he's there?"

Phoenix leaned back in his chair, rubbing his thumb and forefinger over his chin. "Normally, I like to plan things a little better than this, but we've had his girl for over a week, and we don't know where he's got eyes. I don't want to wait around for him to make a move. Let me see that map again." Byte slid the computer to Phoenix. Phoenix studied it closely. He pointed to a spot on the map. "We can stop here to survey the area first. Shaker can set up there to cover us and we'll go ahead on foot."

Phoenix turned to Boar. "You want to go with us? Your Old Lady is welcome to stay here."

Boar sighed. "I wouldn't say I want to, but I will. Let me make sure Shan is okay staying here while we're gone." He paused at the doorway and turned back, "Her sister is secure, right?"

"Shannon can't stumble across her if that's

what you're asking," Phoenix answered. I couldn't help but chuckle. That was true, now that Phoenix had confiscated Reese's lock picking tools. She probably had more, but I knew she wasn't dumb enough to try using them at the clubhouse again.

CHAPTER TWENTY-NINE

Duke

We left the girls at the clubhouse, in the panic room. They were pissed about it, but reluctantly agreed. I don't know what they were complaining about. That damn room was nicer than any other room in the clubhouse. Ranger, Badger, and Dash stayed back with the girls, as well as some prospects and a few other brothers that had just gotten back from a run. They had plenty of protection and should be fine, but I couldn't help worrying about them.

The ride out wasn't bad. It gave me time to clear my head and focus on the task at hand. I couldn't let my mind keep wandering to the fact that my wife and the mother of my child were locked in a panic room together, along with my sister and my son. At least Ember was in there, too; she could kick all of their asses if need be. Regrouping for the hundredth time since we left, I focused on the road and what was to come.

We pulled into a bar in a little town about five miles or so from the cabin. We parked the bikes in the lot and all went inside for a drink. A few brothers stayed to keep up appearances while the rest of us slipped outside one at a time. We loaded up in two cages and continued on toward the cabin.

Phoenix had Coal and Edge driving the cages. They dropped us off on the side of the road with orders to continue driving around the area, but to stay close in case we needed to be picked up ASAP.

We silently trekked through the wooded area to the lookout spot Phoenix had pointed out on the map. It gave us a perfect view of the cabin. I had no idea how in the hell that thing was still standing. There was no way anyone could be using that place as a hideout. Surely, even homeless people would turn their noses up at it.

Phoenix had everyone stay back except for Shaker and himself. They got down on their bellies and started scanning the area. I hated this part, the waiting. I was chomping at the bit to get my hands on this guy and there I was having to wait, quietly, for who knows how long.

Finally, Phoenix put his binoculars down and rolled himself to a sitting position. "Doesn't look like anybody's here." He looked back toward the shack. "I don't think we should go in though. Could be a trap."

Carbon picked up a piece of a branch that had fallen and chucked it toward the house. It fell to the ground, immediately being snapped in half by the sharp teeth of a bear trap. Carbon said wryly, "Yeah, I don't think we should go in either."

Suddenly, gunfire erupted. Bullets were whizzing by and raining down on us from above. Above. What the fuck? We ran for cover, but found little. Standing behind a tree or crouched behind a rock did little to protect you from bullets coming at you from above. That fucker was in the trees.

I poked my head around the tree I was attempting to use for cover and tried to get a visual on the shooter. I saw a thick cloud of smoke around several trees. I poked my head out again, this time looking for the waterfall of casings. Bingo. I aimed the best I could and started firing. When I ran out of bullets, I ducked behind the tree, pulled out my backup piece, and started firing again.

I couldn't tell you if it was me or another brother, but sweet relief washed over me when I saw a body drop from the trees, landing right on another bear trap. Well, if that wasn't karma at her finest. The agonized scream that followed let me know that he was indeed not dead, or at least he wasn't when he fell.

I put my guns away and started looking around for my brothers. I knew from the second the first shot rang out that not all of us would make it out unscathed. I just prayed no one was critically or fatally injured.

I made it back to the clearing to find that my prayers had not been answered favorably. Boar was on the ground, blood pouring from his torso. Phoenix was doing his best to stanch the flow. Carbon was bleeding from his arm, but he was actively helping Phoenix and seemed to be okay. Shaker was on the ground, his body bent over someone, but I couldn't tell who it was. I figured it was Byte since I didn't see him anywhere else.

I ran over to Shaker to see if I could help since Phoenix and Carbon were working on Boar. I looked down and saw Coal lying there, pale and limp. "Where the fuck is Byte?" I barked, my eyes frantically scanning the area for our missing brother.

"He went with Edge to bring the cages closer. When Coal and Edge heard the shots, they came running." He swallowed thickly. "I don't know if—"

"Don't say it, man. Let me help you get him to the cage."

Shaker and I carefully lifted Coal and carried him to the cage. Phoenix and Carbon did the same with Boar. Byte told me to drive so he could find the nearest hospital. I hopped in and floored it, hoping I was headed in the right direction.

CHAPTER THIRTY

Reese

We were shuffled into the panic room while the guys went to handle some "club business." Seriously, they were so transparent. I knew, without a shadow of a doubt, they were going to look for Omen.

Harper's voice interrupted my thoughts. "So, Shannon, how did you meet Boar, if you don't mind me asking?"

I was also dying to know how she ended up as the Old Lady to the president of a motorcycle club that was a quasi-rival to her estranged husband's club.

Shannon smiled wistfully. "We met at a biker rally in Arizona. We were attached at the hip from the moment we met. When the rally was over, he asked me if I wanted to come home with him. I did, and here I am."

"And Melissa? How did she end up in this area?" Harper continued.

Shannon sighed. "A little over a year ago, she had a falling out with our parents, and they cut her off completely. So, she moved out here, claiming she wanted to be close to me, but I've only seen her a handful of times since she arrived."

"How did she hook up with Omen?" I wondered aloud.

"She what?" Shannon asked, clearly surprised.

"Yeah, her and Omen have teamed up, so to speak. You didn't know?"

"No, I didn't know. They met when she came to visit one time, but I had no idea they formed any kind of friendship. I guess I shouldn't be surprised with how fucked up both of them are." She shook her head and pinched the bridge of her nose. "I just don't get it. What are they trying to accomplish?"

"Well, I don't know what Omen's end goal is, but Melissa wanted to kill me and pin James's kidnapping on you so she could have Duke for herself."

Her mouth dropped open for a brief moment and then snapped closed. "I can't believe her. I mean, I can, but really? In what fucked up world would that plan actually work?"

"Yeah, we thought the same thing," I said, gesturing to myself and Harper.

"Hopefully, this will all be over today. It sounds like they're both beyond help," Harper added.

After being cooped up in the panic room for several hours, I was just about out of patience. Dash had been by to check on us frequently and bring me anything I needed for James. You would think being locked in a room with Duke's wife would be what was tipping me over the edge, but it wasn't. Much to my consternation, Shannon was pretty nice, someone I might have been friends with if the circumstances were different. No, it was the fact that for the last two months, I had been locked up in some form or fashion, and I was just damn tired of it.

The buzzer sounded, alerting us that someone was opening the door. I hoped it was to set us free. Ranger walked in with a grave look on his face. "Ladies, we need to get to the hospital quickly. Before you ask, I don't know any details, but we need to get moving."

The four of us filed out of the panic room at a

quick pace. Thankfully, James's diaper bag was fully stocked and ready to go. I just needed to put him in his infant carrier and grab the car seat base.

We rode to the hospital in silence. I hadn't heard from Duke or Carbon, which was tearing up my nerves. Carbon would always text me to let me know he was okay, even when he had no communication orders. After we lost our family, it was imperative for us to know the other was okay. Not hearing from him was not a good sign.

I was so lost in my thoughts, it didn't even dawn on me that we were pulling up to a hospital in Devil Springs. Had we really been in the car that long?

Byte met us at the emergency room doors. Byte, not Duke or Carbon. "Follow me. We've got a private waiting room. I'll fill you in when we get there."

Ember wordlessly walked over and took James from my arms. I looked at her curiously. Did she know something? Was I about to get bad news? She softly said, "My man is right there and has spoken to my dad. Go find out about your man and your brother. I've got James."

I looked around the room. I saw Byte, Edge, and one of Boar's men. "Where the hell is everyone? Start talking, Byte," I snapped.

"Okay, okay. Here's the quick and dirty. We were ambushed with machine gun fire. Phoenix and Carbon were hit, but nothing serious. They are being tended to now. Boar and Coal were hit in the torso, not sure exactly where, but they were both in a bad way when we got here and are now in surgery."

Shannon fell to her knees, sobbing loudly and gasping for breath. Harper crouched down beside her to try to comfort her. She looked up at me with pleading eyes. "Where is Duke?" I demanded.

"He's not hurt. He's either talking with the police or seeing if he can give blood."

"What? Why is he doing that?" I asked.

"Because Coal lost a lot of blood and has a rare blood type. They have some they can use, but the nurse said they prefer to have a match or something like that. Anyway, we all agreed to get tested," Byte explained.

Ember had a funny look on her face. "Where is my dad?"

"He's trying to donate. He's a match, but he was also shot, just a graze, but still, they don't want to let him donate because of it," Byte answered.

"Where do I need to go?" she asked frantically, looking wildly around the room.

"Hey, calm down. I'll show you where you need to go," Byte said.

She handed James back to me. "I'll be back soon."

"Are you okay?" I asked. She didn't look good. She was pale, and I think she was trembling.

"I'm fine. I just...I have the same blood type as my dad. If he's a match, so am I. I need to go so I can help Coal," she rambled and followed Byte out of the room.

Harper was still holding Shannon on the floor, though she didn't miss any of that conversation. "What was that about?" she asked.

"I have no idea. Um, Shannon, I'm going to see if I can find someone to give us an update on Boar, okay?"

She raised her tear-streaked face to look at me, "Please."

I nodded and walked out into the hallway, looking around for the nurse's station. My eyes landed on Duke. I wobbled as fast as I could to him. "Duke!" I shouted.

He opened his arms as soon as he saw me coming. Scooping me up in his arms, he held me close and placed a kiss on the top of my head.

"Sugar," he breathed against the side of my face. He gently placed me back on my feet, but still held me against him.

"Are you okay?" I asked, trying to pull back from him so I could see his face. It was then that I noticed the blood staining his hands and clothes. Gasping, I pointed at the blood and asked, "Is that yours?"

His face dropped. "No, it's Coal's. Shaker and I did the best we could to help him, but I don't know if—" his voice cracked. "He was hurt bad, sugar. He's just a kid, you know? We had him as a driver, to keep him out of harm's way, but him and Edge came running when the shots started. Coal was in front of Edge and took one or two right to the gut. Would have been worse, but when he fell back, Edge took him to the ground and rolled them behind a rock."

"What about the shooter?" I asked softly.

Duke stiffened and pulled me back to him. He cleared his throat, "He's here."

"What?" I shrieked. "Where? Where the fuck is he?" I asked, getting progressively louder.

Duke placed his hand over my mouth. "Shhh! I don't know where he is. He's under arrest and will have a guard with him at all times until he can be discharged from the hospital. It'll be a while, though. He was shot twice, fell from a tree, and landed in a bear trap. Don't know if it was the fall or the trap, or both, but he's paralyzed from the waist down."

"It was Omen, right?" I asked. I knew it was, but I needed to hear it.

"Yeah, sugar, it was."

"Who shot him?" I asked. "I know you aren't supposed to tell me stuff like this, but I need to know, please."

He sighed. "I don't know for sure. He was hit twice, both bullets were .45 ACP, which means it was either your brother or me, or one from each of us."

I nodded. That was enough for me for the time being. "Um, I told Shannon I would come out and see if I could get an update on Boar. Have you heard anything?"

"Yeah, one of the nurses came out about 20 minutes ago and said things weren't as bad as they thought when they originally got in there. She said he was doing okay and should be out of surgery," he looked down at his watch, "any time now."

I tugged on his shirt to get him to lean forward so I could kiss his cheek. "Thanks. I'll be in the waiting room."

I left him where he was and headed back to Shannon. She hugged me tightly when I delivered the update on Boar. "Thank you. Thank you. Thank you." I wasn't sure if she was talking to me, to God, or who knows. She let me go and took a seat in one of the chairs. She straightened and squared her shoulders. "Did someone kill that little bastard?"

I couldn't help myself, I giggled. "I asked almost the exact same thing moments ago." Glancing around the room, I noticed Phoenix had taken a seat near Dash. Phoenix nodded his head once. "Uh, he's in police custody, here at the hospital. He was shot and fell into a bear trap or something. Apparently, he is paralyzed now. In any event, he's going to jail when he gets out of here."

She sighed with relief and almost immediately stiffened again. "What about my sister? She can't be let go."

Phoenix leaned forward and kept his voice low, "She won't be, but let's save that discussion for the clubhouse, yeah?"

She lowered her head. "Yes, of course. My apologies, Phoenix."

Carbon came walking into the waiting room, wearing only his cut over his bare torso. He had a bulky bandage on his upper arm and was holding it close to his body. Before I could ask, he met my eyes and stated, "I'm fine. It's a small flesh wound, but apparently, I'm a bleeder." He shrugged. "How are Coal and Boar? Any word?"

"Boar is doing okay right now, should be coming out of surgery soon. Last I heard, it was still touch and go for Coal. He lost a lot of blood..." Phoenix trailed off, his gaze fixed on the wall.

Just then, Ember rushed through the door, startling everyone in the room. "Daddy! I need to talk to you, in private. Right now!" She was damn near hysterical.

Phoenix stepped into the hallway with Ember. Damn it, he closed the door when he left. I desperately wanted to know what had my friend so upset. Harper leaned forward, "I think I need to use the restroom. Please excuse me."

"Sit your ass down, Harper. You're not going out there to eavesdrop," Carbon ordered.

"Since when do I take orders from you?" she huffed, her plan clearly thwarted.

Carbon smirked. "Since I—"

He was interrupted by Phoenix storming back into the room with Ember right behind him. "Byte, I need you to look up something, like now.

Do you have what you need for that?"

"Depends, Prez. What is it?"

"Birth records," Phoenix said flatly. "For Coal."

"I can probably use my phone for that. I assume he wasn't born as Coal Martin since he was adopted by the Martins. Adoption records are usually sealed with a ridiculous amount of security. You got anything else to go on?" Byte asked.

Phoenix swallowed audibly. "Yeah, can you pull up any records listing Annabelle Burnett as the mother, particularly on the same day Ember was born?"

I sucked in a breath. "Does that mean—?"

Ember turned to face me with tear-filled eyes. "We don't know. He, Dad, and I have the same blood type, and it's rare. When I donated, I found out that Coal and I have the same birthday. He's adopted, he grew up on the farm...it just seems likely that he might be—"

Byte broke in, "He's your brother, your twin brother."

CHAPTER THIRTY-ONE

Duke

I walked into an eerily silent waiting room. Everyone was sitting there with mouths agape, eyes wide, not saying a word. "What happened?" I barked, causing some of the girls to jolt.

"They just found out that Coal is Phoenix's son and Ember's twin brother," Reese said softly.

"What? How do you figure?" I asked.

Ember tried to explain, but she wasn't making any sense. "Blood type, birthday, farm, Mom."

Byte filled in the gaps. "They all have the same rare blood type, he and Ember have the same birthday, he's adopted, he grew up on the farm, and last but not least, his birth mother is listed as Annabelle Burnett on his birth certificate."

"Holy shit," I breathed. "Have you gotten an update on him recently?"

Phoenix shook his head. "No, but I don't think we should tell him about this right away. He doesn't need the shock of it. Oh, fuck me sideways, has anybody called his parents?" His face fell when he realized what he'd just said. He cleared his throat, "Mr. and Mrs. Martin?"

"I did," I said, "right after we got him inside. They should be here soon."

"Thanks, brother. For the time being, let's not mention this to the Martins. Kathleen has had a rough time recently, and this isn't going to be easy for her," Phoenix said.

The waiting room door opened behind me, revealing two uniformed police officers. "Sorry to interrupt. We need to speak with Phoenix Black, William Anderson, John Jackson, and Chase Walker."

Phoenix rose to his feet, striding toward the officers with an outstretched hand. "I'm Phoenix Black. I'm afraid William Anderson is in surgery right now, but the rest of us are here. Shall we step into the hallway?" It wasn't really a question. Phoenix was already using his big body to move them into the hall. "What can we help you with?"

"We actually have a few things we need to share with you. We sent a team out to search the cabin and the surrounding grounds. Thanks for letting us know about the bear traps. They were everywhere. We confiscated 27 illegal traps." The officer cleared his throat and gave Phoenix an appraising look. "You're Copper's cousin, right?"

"Yes, I am."

"And you're a member of Blackwings?"

"I'm the president of the original Blackwings MC chapter. What's that have to do with anything?" Phoenix asked.

"Copper gave me a call when we first started getting the calls about all this. We aren't going to try to pin anything on you; we just need to know what happened, more so to keep things from blowing back on you, you understand?"

Phoenix arched a brow. "Are you saying if I tell you me or one of my boys did something on the wrong side of the law in the name of good that you'll overlook it?"

He nodded. "That's exactly what I'm saying. We've never had any problems with the Blackwings, and I for one appreciate it when you guys take out the trash for us when red tape and such gets in our way."

"All right then, continue," Phoenix said.

"Mr. Allen Anderson is insisting that you're holding his girlfriend in your clubhouse against her will. Is there any truth to that?"

Phoenix rubbed his chin with his thumb and forefinger. "Well, see, about a week ago, someone forced their way onto my private property—my private, gated, and secured property. That person then attacked one of my employees and kidnapped an infant. That infant being John Jackson's son and Chase Walker's nephew. We caught up with the kidnapper and brought them back to the clubhouse. Turns out, the kidnapper was Melissa Massengill. We called her sister to come and get her, but due to personal circumstances, she couldn't come until today. Then, all of this happened. Unfortunately, that hasn't left me with any free time to return to Croftridge to deal with Melissa. If you would like to verify that story, it just so happens that Melissa's sister, Shannon Jackson, also happens to be William Anderson's Old Lady, and she is sitting right there in that waiting room."

"Nothing about that sounds unreasonable to me. You called her sister instead of the authorities because of her mental instability, correct?" the officer coaxed.

"Yes, that's correct. John here knows Melissa

and Shannon from years ago. He was familiar with Melissa's mental history and suggested we call her sister instead of the authorities," Phoenix explained.

"That takes care of that. The reason I called you two out here," he gestured to me and Carbon, "was to let you know that we aren't going to try to determine where the bullets came from. The fact of the matter is, it was a self-defense situation for both of you, and you had every right to shoot him. Your permits were in order, and your guns were registered, so no charges will be filed against either of you."

Carbon and I remained silent, as was our custom when talking with police in the presence of our president. Phoenix always did the talking. "Thanks for letting us know. Did you need us for anything else?" Phoenix asked.

"Not specifically, but I thought you might like to know the team that searched the cabin found much more than expected. Mr. Allen Anderson made the same mistake that most killers make. He did a fantastic job of covering his tracks, but he kept a trophy of sorts from each of his victims. In short, he is responsible for a number of unsolved murders around the area over the years. If he survives his injuries, he'll spend the rest of his life in prison," the officer told us.

That caused Carbon to go against the rules and speak out of turn. "Who did he kill?" he demanded.

"I'm sorry, Mr. Walker, we haven't finished with the investigation and notified the family of the victims. I can't release that information at this time," the officer politely informed him.

Carbon growled low in his throat. Phoenix stepped in front of Carbon and continued talking to the officers. I took a step back and opened the waiting room door. "Reese, now." She didn't question me at all. She got up and came right to me. "Help your brother before he gets arrested."

Reese nodded and squeezed herself between Phoenix and Carbon. Phoenix kept the officers engaged in conversation while Reese spoke softly to Carbon. He whispered something back to her that made her entire body stiffen. She slowly pivoted her body as one solid unit. It was the eeriest thing I had ever seen. She said in a very robotic, monotone voice. "I'm Reese Walker and this is my brother, Chase Walker. We are the next of kin for James Walker, Heather Walker, Mason Walker, Sage Walker, and Ruby Walker."

The officer's face blanched. He looked to his partner who had been silent the entire time. The partner stepped forward and nodded his head. "Allen Anderson is responsible for the murder of your mother, father, brother, sister, and grandmother."

I braced myself for the fallout, hoping like hell Carbon would be easier to contain with a wounded arm. The big man sank to his knees and pulled his sister to him with his good arm. His body shook with silent sobs while Reese allowed her cries to be heard. When I heard Carbon say, "We got him, Reesie. It's finally over," I knew their tears were tears of relief.

"Thank you, officers. They needed that more than you will ever know," Phoenix said, extending his hand to them.

A man in light blue scrubs approached our group. "Excuse me, I'm looking for the family of Coal Martin."

Phoenix cleared his throat, "That's me."

"May I speak freely here?" the doctor asked. Phoenix nodded. "Mr. Martin is out of surgery and in recovery. We will need to keep him for a few days. He's a very lucky man. We removed three bullets and got the bleeding under control. The bullets didn't hit any major organs, but they did significant damage to several of the larger vessels in the abdomen. Had he not gotten here when he did— Well, it was touch-and-go there at first, but he stabilized and pulled through. You can see him as soon as he is moved to a room."

"Thank you, doctor," Phoenix said, reaching out to shake his hand.

The first officer cleared his throat to get our attention. "We'll let you get back to your family and friends. We have all we need from you for now, and we know how to get in touch with you if we need anything. Thanks for helping us out on this one."

We had just entered the waiting room when another doctor came in. "Family of William Anderson." Shannon stood and followed him into the hallway. She returned a few minutes later to tell us that Boar made it through surgery and was being moved to the ICU.

Thinking I would have a few minutes of reprieve, I dropped my ass into a chair and pulled Reese into my lap. Not even two minutes later, Copper showed up. I swear the room was busier than Grand Central Station. "You folks need a place to stay tonight?" he asked.

Sounds of agreement echoed through the room. "Me and a couple of the guys brought some cages up here. We can take some folks back to the clubhouse if anyone wants to leave. I'll leave two cages here in case some of you want to stay and need transportation handy."

Phoenix walked over to Copper and pulled him into a bear hug. "Thanks, brother. You've been a Godsend every step of the way this past year. Appreciate it."

Copper gasped in mock outrage. "Who let Phoenix grow a pussy?"

"Fucker," Phoenix shot back and clipped his shoulder.

I patted Reese's thigh to get her to stand, "Come on, sugar, let's take James to the clubhouse. I need a shower and about 20 hours of sleep."

EPILOGUE

Duke

"Reese! Let's go! We're going to be late!" I shouted up the stairs. She had been in the bathroom for over an hour getting ready for a party at the clubhouse. I had no idea what was taking her so long, but I had been ready to go for well over 30 minutes.

She came down the stairs looking just as gorgeous as she always did. "Calm down, I'm ready. I just wanted to make sure I looked nice."

I gave her a quick peck on the cheek. "You always look nice, sugar."

She rolled her eyes. "Yeah, yeah, but tonight is different. This is the first time I've ever been to a patch-in party, and it will be the first party I attend as your Old Lady. Sue me for wanting to look good."

"Shut it, Reese, and get your ass on my bike," I growled and swatted said ass.

Reese and I moved in together pretty much as soon as we returned to Croftridge. She asked to see written proof of my divorce before she agreed to move in with me. Thankfully, all I had to do was file the papers, and it was a done deal.

There was an empty house on Phoenix's farm property that he said we could rent for a steal. I didn't think Reese would go for it, but she did. She said she didn't want to live on the farm forever, but it was okay for the time being. It was close to Ember and Mrs. Martin, both of whom loved to babysit James.

I thought it might take some time for Reese to be comfortable leaving James with a babysitter again, but she was surprisingly okay with it. Of course, that might be because the culprits who orchestrated our son's kidnapping would never be a threat to his safety again.

Omen was found dead in his hospital bed a few days after everything went down. Thankfully, it was after Coal had been discharged, and no Blackwings were anywhere near the hospital. Boar, however, was still there. We'll never know, but I personally believe Boar was behind Omen's death.

Melissa was arrested for numerous crimes. I have no doubt some strings were pulled and favors called in because it was quickly decided she was mentally incompetent to stand trial. She'll be reevaluated periodically, but, as I understood it, she'll never be found competent and will spend the rest of her days in the maximum security wing of the state mental hospital.

My musings came to an end when we pulled through the gates of the clubhouse. As expected, the place was packed. We had parties almost every weekend, but this particular party was special. The president's son was being patched in.

After Coal was discharged from the hospital, Phoenix and the Martins sat down and told him about his biological parents. Having known about his adoption from an early age, he took the news in stride. Regardless of his paternity, he was receiving his patch just shy of a year prospecting because he risked his life when he charged into the line of fire to help his brothers.

Fingers snapped in front of my face. "Did you hear me?" Reese asked, clearly annoyed with my lack of attention.

"Sorry, sugar. What did you say?"

She smiled. "I said I'm ready for you to take me in there as your Old Lady."

I laughed. "Sugar, they've known you were my Old Lady for a while now."

She playfully slapped my chest. "Don't rain on my parade. I want to make a grand entrance."

I grabbed her arm and pulled her to me. "I love you, Reese Walker."

"I love you, too, Duke Jackson."

Phoenix

I was fucking exhausted after Coal's patch-in party, but I had work to do. In addition to my regular club responsibilities, I spent several hours a day going through the shit we found hidden all over the farm. Boxes upon boxes of files and folders. Octavius kept meticulous records. It had taken me almost a year to get through the better part of it, and I still had nothing on Annabelle.

I tossed the current papers I was holding into the shredder and moved to the next folder in the stack. When I opened it, my breath caught in my chest. I closed my eyes and slowly opened them again, not believing what I was seeing. At the top of the first paper in the folder was the name I had been searching for. Annabelle Burnett.

My hands were shaking as I carefully placed the folder on my desk and began looking through it. My heart was pounding in my chest, blood whooshing in my ears as I looked at the contents of the folder. The first things I saw were Annabelle's birth certificate and social security card. Then, birth records for Ember, Coal, and Nivan. Nivan's death certificate. But it was the next few papers that changed everything. "Fucking finally," I said as I reached for my phone.

Also by Teagan Brooks

Blackwings MC
Duke
Phoenix
Carbon
Shaker